The Mountain's Child

Connie Kruger

New Generation Publishing

Disclaimer

This novel is entirely a work of fiction. The names, characters and incidents portrayed in it are the work of the authors' imagination. Any resemblance to actual persons, living or dead, events or locations, is entirely coincidental.

About the Author

Connie Kruger was born and brought up in South Africa, where she studied psychology and criminology at the University of South Africa. While raising her son and working as a librarian she wrote short stories and poems, which were published in various magazines. In 1984 she and her family moved to the UK. This was quite an adjustment and she found solace in writing humorous sketches on her daily life as a mother and housewife in England. These were broadcast as a series by the South Africa Broadcasting Corporation. Once settled in her new environment she continued to write, producing two novels and a children's story. She considered this time an apprenticeship in her craft. Then she embarked on a new career.

In 1993 she saw there was an opportunity for her to build on her psychology degree by qualifying as a Person Centred counsellor and supervisor. She worked in this field for over a decade: in the National Health Service, counselling and supporting NHS staff; as the practice counsellor in a GP surgery; in colleges, supervising trainee counsellors; and in private practice.

On her retirement she re-visited South Africa, travelled to India and Ireland attending courses where she could explore those parts of herself, which lay beyond the mind. This travelling inspired 'The Mountain's Child'.

Connie lived in The Lake District for nearly two decades, where this book was written. She recently moved to West Sussex to be closer to her family.

ACKNOWLEDGEMENTS

I would like to acknowledge and thank the following people:

My lovely son and daughter-in-law Alexander and Rebecca Beveridge, were the first and repeated readers of my manuscript. Their enthusiasm, encouragement and continuing feedback gave me the confidence to show it to others: Jenny Walter, Chris Gibbs and Sue Naylor, who all added valuable practical input. Fran Leaver, and Brenda Mean read my manuscript and spurred me on to publish. Gordon and Sylvia Price showed consistent interest in my publishing journey, always providing encouragement and support. Sylvia also gifted me with the big task of proofreading. Com O'Malley gifted a final proofread when the manuscript was in book format and suggested ways of promoting the novel.

Finally a special thank you to my editor Sally Orson-Jones without whose expertise and guidance 'The Mountain's Child' might never have fully emerged from the mist.

For my grandsons:
Henry, Frederick and Oliver
who have wonderful parents.

PROLOGUE

<u>KwaZulu-Natal, South Africa, 2004</u>

The mountain, edged against the vast African sky, snaked its huge bulk all around the valley. Proud and clear, seemingly impassive, it towered over the human dramas below. Yet it had a moodiness of its own, often hiding, pulling a veil of mist over its jagged head. The sun would tear this away not long after the people from the huts down in the valley had made their way up to the big brick houses where the white people lived, and where they earned their living. At times the mountain could hide for days on end, and then no one could see that peculiar upright rock which, if looked at with the inner gaze, resembled an old man with a beard.

One hot January morning, long before the sun could colour the mountain, or had even lit the sky, the slender girl was awoken by the contractions in her stomach. She knew her time had come. She drew the curtain separating her 'room' from that of the old woman who lay on her back snoring, mouth wide open, displaying what stumps of teeth she had left.

"Auntie!"

The snoring stopped.

"Auntie, it's my time."

The old woman opened her eyes, wiped her hand over her face, and got up. There was no fuss. She had delivered many a baby into a world of hunger and disease, to live for a few months, a few years, longer sometimes. Long enough to serve at some big house somewhere under the watching eye of the mountain.

The mountain was still veiled when the first cry pierced the silence. The old woman looked aghast at the perfectly formed little girl.

"She's nearly white!"

The girl didn't answer and the large luminous eyes in her dark face gave nothing away; the wind whispering secrets through the crevices in the walls was all that could be heard.

The old woman stared at her. "Ayish" she shook her head, then continued with her work. When she had finished and the baby rested in her mother's arms, she picked up the bowl of reddish brown water and made for the door muttering under her breath: "Apartheid finished long time, but still no food, no jobs, nothing," she pursed her lips. Outside she emptied the liquid on the parched soil where she knew the midday sun would suck up every drop of it.

That evening when the girl sat by the fire under the starlit sky, nursing her baby with one arm, the hand of the other exploring the little feet, the tiny fingers, stroking the precious head gently, she spoke to the old woman.

"Tomorrow, first light, I'll put her by the door of the white people."

A gust of wind swept across the fire, blowing a screen of smoke across the girls face, hiding her tears. The old woman looked hard at her.

"You give your child away?"

The girl bent her head towards the treasured bundle in her arms. One obstinate tear escaped and plopped – right onto the baby's heart.

"She'll eat." Her voice was wobbling.

"Perhaps they beat her, they'll make her work for them for nothing."

"She'll eat. She'll grow. She will *live*." Her words were strong now, almost a proclamation.

The old woman was silent. There was nothing to say; she'd seen too many babies die. For a while the crackling of the fire was the only conversation between the two women. The smell of freshly cooked crumble porridge filled the air. When they stuck their fingers into the shared bowl of food, the old woman spoke again.

"And you, will you go see her sometimes?"

The girl shuddered, clasping the baby tightly to her chest. She shook her head.

"I'll take the Thursday bus out of the valley."

The old woman raised her eyebrows, the question in her eyes.

"I'll go to the big city. I'll find work."

The old woman gave a deep sigh. "Ayish".

CHAPTER 1

When Bruno Mynhard woke up on that mellow spring morning and tried to move his right arm, the vague fear that had been hovering in the back of his consciousness for years now turned into terror.

The arm would not move!

He tried again. But now even the tingling sensation that had been coming and going so menacingly, and which had plagued him constantly over the last four weeks, was gone. There was nothing there, no movement, no life. Nothing.

With his left hand, he gently raised the paralysed arm as one would the corpse of a beloved child. He held it close to his chest for a long time, stroking the forearm hairs to one side, then to the other.

So, it has happened. Even though the tingling and sudden weaknesses followed by periods of remission had warned him that the loss was imminent, it still came as a shock. Could there, even now, be a remission?

He knew there wouldn't be.

He moved himself into a sitting position and the dead arm fell off his chest. He picked it up again and then, with a violent movement, pushed it away from his body. Anger flooded him. Why him? It wasn't fair! Had he not lost enough? Slowly over the years his legs had deteriorated so that now he had to move around the house in a wheelchair. To go around his smallholding to see if Filamon had carried out his instructions properly he had to get into his electric buggy - he had had two working arms then.

He heard Filamon whistling at the hen pen, and he could imagine him holding the tin bucket with one hand while sprinkling the feed with the other to the excitedly cackling birds. He could see him sitting beside Witvlies, extracting rich creamy milk from her udder while chanting a Zulu song in a deep baritone voice. He could see him digging the vegetable garden, tenderly putting the young plants into the rich red soil, watering, harvesting in the autumn. Filamon had two working arms and legs that could gobble up mile after mile when he went visiting his family who lived far away.

The gall rose up in Bruno. He puckered his thin lips, causing a deep frown above his well-proportioned nose, distorting his fine features. He wanted to shout out those bitter feelings, but automatically he suppressed them, as he had done for so many years now. He felt the shivers go through him and pulled the blankets up with his strong arm. He needed more now than only Katrina coming in daily, there was no denying it. He sat with that thought for a long time. Late that afternoon he picked up the phone, his hand shaking, and phoned his sister Kate de Wit.

Miriam knew her place in the de Wit household, and in the wider community. This understanding had come to her gradually as she grew up, and she often longed for the time before she was aware of it; that magical time when she first managed to totter off into the garden chasing the light spots that the foliage of the trees had allowed the sun to make on the grass. She shrieked gleefully as she grabbed them, feeling her hands full of light, yet being amazed that the spots were on the ground as well. She saw tiny winged creatures dancing in and around the flowers beckoning her to come and play, and when she got there, they were gone. She lay flat on her tummy, inching her way forward, searching for them. She knew they were there because she could hear their laughter, but when she got close to their sound it turned into bird song. The notes the birds seemed to pour into the air all around her would fascinate her.

She was aware of friendly faces too, looking at her, talking to her; several faces, but one face was there constantly. When she woke up in the morning or from her afternoon nap, this friendly loving face hovered over her, seeing to her needs. That same face put her to bed at night and stayed with her until sleep took her into a world of gold winged creatures singing even more beautifully than the birds.

Gradually she came to know the names of the faces around her. The one who tended to her so lovingly and with whom she stayed at night, was Aunty Lizzie. She had thick black hair, which cascaded down onto her shoulders when she brushed it out. Mostly though it was tied up away from her smiling dark eyes so that she could laugh into them, joyously, when Aunty Lizzie's playful brown hands tickled her tummy. Aunty Lizzie's smooth and youthful skin was like hers, not quite white, but not black like the farm-workers either. The hard painted face one she was told to call Mrs. de Wit, and the two children's names she learned were Sandra and Bessie. The face with the hair on his upper lip she called Mr. de Wit.

She couldn't remember when she realized that Sandra and Bessie called Mr. and Mrs. de Wit Mummy and Daddy, and when they talked about them they said 'my Mummy and Daddy' as if they belonged to them. But there was no one who *she* called Mummy, or who she could talk about as 'my Mummy'.

That puzzled her so she asked Aunty Lizzie:

"Are you my Mummy?"

She saw sadness in Aunty Lizzie's eyes when she shook her head and said:

"No. I wish I was."

"Who is my Mummy?" she asked.

Aunty Lizzie had looked at the hissing primus stove for a while before she answered.

"We don't know, Miriam."

"Why?"

She sighed. "Mr. de Wit found you on the front doorstep one morning when he went out to go to work."

Miriam couldn't make that out.

"Why?" she asked again.

"Oh Miriam, stop asking why!" Aunty Lizzie sounded upset. "All you need to know is that I love you as if you were my own child." She came and put her hand on Miriam's head, "and God loves you and always will."

That pleased her. She knew that Aunty Lizzie loved her, but to have God, where ever he was, loving her too, felt good.

When she was older she was given the job of polishing all the shoes in the house and she believed that she could make them shine better than anyone else could. One day Bessie threw her shoe at her and shouted: "Polish it properly! Buff up those streaks at the heel." She felt like throwing the shoe in Bessie's face, but Bessie towered over her. She knew that Bessie's size didn't really matter, she just didn't dare say anything rude to her, because she had Mr. and Mrs. de Wit for a mummy and daddy and she, Miriam, had no mummy or daddy. Luckily Sandra came in and said, "Now, now Bessie, she's only a child, don't take your PMT out on her."

She didn't know what PMT was, and she didn't care either, all she wanted to do was to get out of that room and go to Aunty Lizzie. But Aunty Lizzie wasn't at home. Mrs. De Wit had taken her along to the shops to help her with the tons of shopping that came into the house every month. So she buffed Bessie's shoes up again, making sure she didn't miss any bits, and then ran out of the house to cry.

The sun was bright on the peaks and there, in between two large ones, she saw the rock that looked like an old man with a beard. Looking at it with her eyes full of tears she remembered that when Mr. de Wit took them to church, the preacher read from the Bible about Moses who met God on the mountain, and that God had spoken to him. Standing there, blinking against the sun, she thought that God had come to console her.

"God," she said, "Bessie threw her shoe at me like I'm a bit of rubbish! And I can't even shout back at her because, one day when I was very angry and stamped my foot, Aunty Lizzie told me to always be a good girl, otherwise Mr. and Mrs. de Wit might send me to the orphanage. God, I never want to be away from Aunty Lizzie."

She felt that although God was silent He was listening to her. Then it struck her that if God loved her, as Aunty Lizzie said he did, He could be her father. She was excited by the idea. Bessie could throw her shoes at her, and Sandra could make her fetch this and that for her, but really she, Miriam, was the winner, because Mr. and Mrs. de Wit could never, ever be such loving parents as Aunty Lizzie and God.

That evening when she and Aunty Lizzie were sitting around the primus stove in their two-roomed prefab house, she told her all that. Aunty Lizzie hugged and hugged her, then told her that when she was a baby, everyone in the big house had a hand in bringing her up.

"Bessie and Sandra adored you, and played with you whenever they could sneak away from their homework."

Aunty Lizzie went very serious when she said:

"You are blessed Miriam, always remember that it was through the kindness of Mr. de Wit's heart that we could keep you."

Miriam thought about what she had said, and about Mr. and Mrs. de Wit. She had always liked Mr. de Wit. It was his eyes that she liked best. Not their colour, they were only a measly blue, but what was inside them. When he looked at her, she always thought his eyes were smiling, even if his mouth wasn't. He spoke quietly, not like the other big-tummy Afrikaner men who sometimes visited the house bellowing out their greetings, slapping Mr. de Wit on the back. Nor like Mrs. de Wit whose voice sounded harsh as she pushed the words out through her scarlet lips. No, his voice was friendly, always, even when he told her not to trample on the plants in the flowerbeds. But Mrs. de Wit, well the only thing she liked about her was the colour of the blouses she wore. She ironed them every week: orange, brown, pink and tan, and the deep sky blue one with the white specks in it.

It wasn't as if Mrs. de Wit did horrible things to her - oh no, she always made sure she and Aunty Lizzie had enough to eat, and that she had enough clothes. It was really just her eyes. They always looked at her as if they didn't see her, and they didn't smile like Mr. de Wit's. Miriam saw hardness deep inside them. Bessie looked like her mother, except her hair was black. Sandra had Mr. de Wit's light brown hair, but her eyes were a beautiful blue, a real deep colour, which sparkled when she laughed. She had a clear memory of Sandra giving her a piggyback, galloping like a horse until she shrieked with laughter. That was when she was quite little.

School holidays were busy times for her and Aunty Lizzie. Usually Sandra and Bessie brought friends home to stay, and there were many beds to make and the biggest pans in the kitchen came out of the cupboards to cook in. One time Mrs. de Wit's old brother Mr. Mynhard, came too. She didn't like him much even though he was friendly to her. She saw that he had grey hair that hung around a large bald patch on the top of his head. Because his face looked funny to her, she kept looking at it to try and make out why. She didn't think he would notice her staring at him, because his brown eyes kept shifting about all the time he spoke to people, never really looking at them. After a while she could make out why his face looked so strange. It was that frown of his; it looked as if it was running from his forehead right into the bald patch. It made him look very angry, but his voice didn't sound angry when he spoke to her.

"I hear you do well at school, Miriam."

"Yes sir," she said.

"My name is Bruno, Miriam."

She didn't think she could call him Uncle Bruno, like Sandra and Bessie, so she said:

"Yes Mr. Bruno."

He smiled, and the frown was only holding on to the bald patch. He got up heavily, leaning on the dining room table, which Aunty Lizzie was starting to lay for dinner.

"I hear she could read and write before she went to school, Lizzie," he said "no doubt due to your efforts."

Aunty Lizzie's light brown face coloured pink and her eyes sparkled.

"I tried to help, Mr. Mynhard."

"Hmm," he said, and shuffled towards his wheelchair, gripping his walking stick firmly.

That evening when she and Aunty Lizzie had at last done the big pile of washing up and swept the kitchen, they took their food, which was being kept warm in the pans on the stove, and went to their little house. Miriam thought that Aunty Lizzie was really pleased with what Mr. Bruno had said to her, because she started telling her how clever he was.

"He was headmaster of a big school in Cape Town before he came here to KwaZulu-Natal, you know, Miriam."

"Bigger than my school, Aunty Lizzie?"

Aunty Lizzie laughed. "Oh, that school could swallow up Rusthof Primary five times."

That put Miriam off him even more. She thought that he must be a very cruel man to have a school that would swallow up her little school where she was so happy. There were two large classrooms for the fifty of them, boys and girls together, an office and a tearoom. But best of all was the green field stretching out all around the building, sprouting yellow flowers in the early spring. She loved the smell of freshly cut grass when the black man, called Petrus, pushed the mower across it, singing high notes, then making deep low sounds when he did his little jigs.

When Aunty Lizzie spoke again her voice was very sad, "Mr. Mynhard had a little girl who died when she was just eight years old; poor Mr. Mynhard."

Miriam felt sorry for the poor little girl who could no longer skip in the sunshine or go to school any more. School was such a good place! There was no housework to help with; there were playmates, and she got lots of praise from Miss Lang their teacher. Miss Lang had blond hair, and Miriam noticed how well it toned in with the brown of her eyes. Her skin was very white, and Aunty Lizzie told her that that was because she came from England.

"Why?" Miriam was puzzled. "Why did England make her skin so white?"

"Oh, I guess it's because they don't get as much sun over there as we have here in South Africa."

She stroked Aunty Lizzie's arm. "Why did the sun make our skins so much darker than Sandra and Bessie's?"

Aunty Lizzie laughed out loud. "No, that was not the sun Miriam."

"What was it then?"

Aunty Lizzie paused for a moment before she spoke. "You see, white people have two white parents, and black people have two black parents. People with our sort of skin colour have one white and one black parent, or sometimes the black and white mixing happened already with our grandparents or even great, great grandparents, and that's what makes our skins darker than the white people's."

"Oh."

"We are called coloureds."

She was the only coloured child in the school. There were no black children. Aunty Lizzie said their parents couldn't afford the school fees.

Miriam always felt that Miss Lang was smiling at her especially nicely, and she was praised a lot.

"What a lovely picture you painted Miriam! Oh I do I like the colours you've put together." Often Miss Lang would put her pictures up on the display board.

Miss Lang was the only teacher Miriam had during her years in that small rural school, and that she thought was really lucky. After her first two years with Miss Lang, she was supposed to move up to Mr. Brink's class, and she had been dreading that. Mr. Brink had a cane, which he swivelled around as he spoke to the children during assembly, then swished it against his breeches so that it just missed his shoes. Miriam could not remember him ever smiling at her, but he was always very cordial towards Mr. de Wit when he dropped her off at school before taking Sandra and Bessie into town to the High School. He would say something like, 'See you at the match on Saturday Daniel.' To Miriam, he never said a word; he scarcely looked at her.

She often wondered what happened to that cane of his after his heart attack, which had led to his early retirement. But what ever happened to it, she was free of its threatening presence, and of Mr. Brink. Miss Lang was moved up to teach the next level and their whole class moved up with her.

She had several playmates at school, and they skipped together, played hopscotch, and sniggered at the boys behind their backs, yet none of her friends ever asked her to come and sleep over at their homes, and she couldn't invite them over either. Where would they sleep? With her and Aunty Lizzie? Alone in a room in the de Wit's house? What was the fun in that? It just wasn't going to work out. So she watched them making their arrangements with each other while the sense of separateness, the feeling of being different and alone, lay heavily in her heart.

Still that was better than what was to come.

Bruno Mynhard learned early on in his life that violence was not acceptable, at least not from him. That prerogative belonged to his father, that man, with his uniform and decorations, who came into his life when he was four years old. There was great excitement when the family prepared for this homecoming.

"You can be really proud of your father," his grandma had said. "He helped rid the world of the Nazis."

He had heard much talk about the war and the Nazis. Nazis – a word that was spat out with venom by the women whose men went up north, as the expedition into North Africa was referred to. The families who opposed the Afrikaners joining British forces spat the word 'joiners' out with equal venom. 'It was but yesterday that they invaded us, and took our land, destroyed our farms and livelihood, and now you go and fight with them! Shame on you!' Sometimes they would punctuate their feelings of disgust with a well-aimed stream of spit to land right at the feet of the 'joiner'.

Those days in the Transvaal, as it was called then, violence was in the very air one breathed in.

Inside the house, with his doting mother and grandmother, Bruno felt safe. Until, that is, his father came home. He expected this heroic man who lifted him high onto his shoulders and exclaimed, "So this is my son, my very own lad who will follow in my footsteps!" to be as doting and gentle with him as his mother and grandmother. But that jubilant meeting between father and son lasted no longer then a few days. Gone were the early mornings snuggled up in his mother's bed. He felt kicked out by this burly soldier against whom he had no defence. Yet Bruno had the warrior spirit in him, and when one day in the kitchen, his father shouted at his mother, he stood up for her, all four years of him.

"Don't you dare shout at my Mummy!"

That was when Bruno first learned that violence was the prerogative of his father, and that he could be squashed like an ant if he expressed his anger. Soon enough though he understood that home could be a dangerous place even without him showing his resentment. He sought refuge in his grandmother's house more and more over those years when three stillborn baby boys were born, and his father took it as a personal insult that the sons he begot 'do not care to stay with me.' He was walking on eggshells; or was it on a cobweb over a precipice? Either way, he could not win, and the anger he felt had to be buried so deep that not even he could find it.

He was nearly fifteen when Kate was born, bouncing into the world with gusto. His father marvelled at her appetite and rosy cheeks, and doted on her. So did Bruno and his mother. She had restored some semblance of peace in the home and his father's bouts with the bottle stopped for a while.

The other thing Bruno learned as he grew up was that alcohol could make a man talk about deep things, hidden things. One evening when they all sat watching the glowing coals of the barbeque after a huge helping of pork chops and new potatoes, when the ex soldier had downed more beer than usual - that evening Bruno learned why it was that he never had any contact with his paternal grand parents, and that his father had left home at the age of sixteen.

"She was a vixen, red hair and all. God knows why he had to go and marry her after my mother died. She wanted everything *her* way, in *my* mother's house! I told her straight." The bitterness engulfed the word 'her'. "And of course immediately she ran to my father with the tears streaming down that freckled face."

Bruno was intrigued.

"And what did grandpa do?"

His father was silent for some time staring into the fire where sparkling coals shot out burning sparks. It was when Bruno thought that he had lost track of his own conversation that his voice came through, thick with emotion:

"I had to go down to the river to wash my blood caked clothes off me." His father's chest was heaving, and when he spoke again the tears were sitting in his voice. "A whip can cut deep wounds. They wouldn't let me into the house when I refused to apologize to her."

Bruno sat quite still, wondering whether to probe further. But his father's voice slurred on,

"I never went back, never saw him again. Years later, when he lay dying, he sent for me, but I refused to go."

His father sat hunched up for a long time, and this time Bruno did not wonder whether he should probe or not. This was a moment between his father and his conscience. His mother did not speak either. Only the crickets celebrated the night, singing to the stars, dotted like jewels in the cloudless sky. A full moon slowly rose above the Magaliesberg mountain range, as they rolled on mile after mile across the bone-dry grassland.

At last his father straightened himself up proudly.

"I am a self made man Bruno. I taught myself English with the help of a dictionary, and today I am a man who has been decorated for bravery in the war. Do you understand?"

"Yes dad," Bruno said, "I understand very well."

He did not know exactly what it was that he understood, but he knew that on some deep, almost cellular level, his ancestral history had relayed the message: it was very dangerous to express the anger and resentment he felt towards his father or to anyone else, ever.

When Bruno passed his matric with flying colours, his father seemed proud to put up the money for his university education and shook his hand warmly at his graduation ceremony. Shortly after that he died suddenly of a stroke, and Bruno was left with a sense of relief, which made him feel guilty. But the pattern of dealing with that kind of feeling had been established: there was space in the coffin that housed his anger. The guilt simply slipped away from his consciousness.

When the blow struck there was no time or possibility for Miriam, or Aunty Lizzie, to ward it off. It fell upon them out of the blue. For Miriam, literally out of a blue sky. It was one of those times when the mountain had been hiding behind a veil all week long, and Miriam was longing to see God again. On that fateful morning she knew as soon as she peeped through the opening in the curtains that he would be there. So she pulled her clothes on hastily and slipped quietly out of the bedroom so not to wake Aunty Lizzie.

The air was crisp and clear, and the sun was just beginning to stroke the sky. It was the best time of the day, and she loved going out into the garden to sit under the big wild fig tree and watch the rose and blue above the mountain folding themselves into each other's arms, and to see God. Especially on a Saturday when she didn't have to rush off to school. Sure enough, there he was, standing erect between the two peaks, his long beard flowing into his robes. She just sat staring at him, not really knowing what to chat to him about. She was feeling very still inside herself after the night's sleep. So she just sat there, half dozing, drinking in her beloved mountain, God's home.

It was then that it happened.

The voice in her head was clear: *Be strong, it is as it is. You are loved and always will be loved.*

She opened her eyes wide and shuddered. What was this? Was she dreaming? Or was this God speaking to her? He had never spoken to her, but she always felt he was listening to her, hearing every word she said. She closed her eyes and sat puzzling over the words for a long time; then, unexpectedly, her mind wondered off to what she had overheard the night before when, at dusk, she passed Mr. And Mrs. De Wit's wide open bedroom window.

Mr. De Wit was talking and she could hear the concern in his voice – it had that compassionate tone to it.

"Gosh! He can't live on his own now; especially at night. He will need someone to sleep in."

"But who?" The usual shrillness of Mrs. De Wit's voice had climbed a pitch higher and Miriam could tell she was worried. "You know how finicky he is, everything in his house has to be just so, and his food has to be cooked in a very specific way."

"Well Katrina can't sleep in, she has her children waiting for her at home. It has to be someone without family commitments, a youngster perhaps, one of the many unemployed." Mr. de Wit hesitated. "But will he be satisfied?"

His voice had become louder and Miriam realized that he had moved closer to the open window. She quickly ducked so that the bushy shrubs could hide her and then crept away quietly. She felt guilty for eavesdropping, so decided to just forget about it and not tell Aunty Lizzie.

But now the thoughts were there again – and this voice she has heard! What does it all mean? She felt a chill in her bones and pulled her cardigan close around her body. Should she tell God about it? She opened her eyes and looked at the mountain, but God had vanished. A black cloud had swallowed up half the mountain, flashing furiously, like a snake's tongue before striking. It was one of those sudden unexpected thunderstorms, and the rain came galloping down the mountain. She jumped up and ran. She reached the house just as a grey curtain of rain engulfed everything, and the sky boomed out cannon fire.

She realized that she must have sat under the tree longer than she thought, because the grown-ups were up already and Aunty Lizzie was clearing away the breakfast dishes. She went into the kitchen and started at the sink full of saucepans. The door leading to the dining room was open and she could hear Mrs. de Wit speaking to Aunty Lizzie.

"Lizzie, I had news from my brother. He's not getting better."

Aunty Lizzie clicked her tongue. "I'm sorry to hear, Mrs. de Wit!"

Miriam stopped washing up and went into the dining room.

"He needs help, Lizzie. His right arm has gone lame, he can't move it now."

"Oh!" Aunty Lizzie's dark eyes grew large; "it might get better again."

Mrs. de Wit shook her head. "I don't think so Lizzie, from now on it can only get worse."

Mrs. de Wit turned and looked at Miriam.

"Miriam's a big girl now, and she's so clever with the housework. Aren't you Miriam?"

Miriam saw Aunty Lizzie's light brown skin pale, and as she felt her stomach drop through to her bowels, she remembered the clear voice that had come into her head earlier on.

Without waiting for an answer from her, Mrs. de Wit turned back to Aunty Lizzie. "He needs help urgently. I told Mr. Mynhard we'll bring Miriam over next week-end. It may only be a temporary arrangement until we can sort out something else".

Aunty Lizzie's eyes were saucers now and her hand, holding the tablecloth was shaking.

"But Miriam is only twelve, how can she leave her school?"

"We've thought about that Lizzie, Mr. Mynhard will teach her. You know he was a schoolteacher before he retired. It will give him something to do."

"But Mrs. de Wit, please, Miriam is my…" Aunty Lizzie stopped and swallowed. "She'll have no friends there, she'll be…"

"Look, Lizzie," Mrs. de Wit's voice was unbending, "we are doing the best for this child. You know yourself what poor facilities Rusthof has. One teacher having to deal with several levels of education, and no computers! No broadband!" She waved a hand at the mountain, "These blooming peaks, it's bad enough that Sandra and Bessie have to go to the library in town to do their IT work! Miriam should be grateful for the opportunity of private education. She's far too clever for the bunch at Rusthof any way."

Miriam saw Aunty Lizzie's mouth open like a fish caught on a hook, gasping for words, but nothing came out. She looked ashen as if she could faint at any moment. Mrs. De Wit moved closer to her and touched her hand slightly.

"You'll be able to go and see her on your off week-ends Lizzie." She turned away from Aunty Lizzie who just stood there like a corpse, not responding. "It may only be for a year or so," she said as she picked up her car keys and reached for her handbag.

CHAPTER 2

Lizzie Aaronson had never known a time when there wasn't a mountain in her life. She was born in one of the valleys the Outeniqua mountain range had carved out, to parents who moved from rented room to rented room, always living in other people's homes. Bowing and scraping, ingratiating themselves in order not to be kicked out was the norm. When they were in arrears with the rent or when her dad had come in drunk on an evening and sung rude songs loudly, and her mother was unable to quiet him down, she could see them packing their meagre belongings into cardboard boxes again.

Lizzie was the eldest and the only child for six years, before three siblings followed in short succession. That was during the time when her dad came home drunk often. First Samuel, then Sarah and finally Bennet. Lizzie was only fifteen when she was put into service. She was lucky. Her schoolteacher, who spotted her intelligence, felt it a great shame that she had to leave school. He had an aunt in Cape Town who worked for extremely well to do people as housekeeper. She was going to retire in a year's time and the lady of the house was looking for someone suitable whom she could train up to the standards of that household. Lizzie with her bright eyes, ready smile and neat figure found favour and was taken on. She tied her thick black hair up, out of the way, and donned her housemaid's cap. In that colossal house she not only learned all the intricacies of housekeeping, but importantly, she learned to drop the way they spoke at home and adopt the accent and manner of speech of her employers. That was a requirement of her mistress, Mrs. de Waal.

Many parcels were delivered to that household, and one day when there was a dispute about the delivery of a consignment of vintage wines, Mrs. de Waal demanded that the manager of the store himself came out to see 'what rubbish you have sent me.'

Joshua arrived in style. Mercedes Benz shining like a mirror, dark striped suit and flashy tie; shoes that looked like they could just slip onto the dance floor never ever to put a foot wrong.

Lizzie watched him from a window on the top floor as he got out. He had pitch-black wavy hair, green eyes, and a swarthy skin. Her body suddenly felt very alive and she went downstairs to find some unknown object she had 'mislaid'. Joshua was charm itself to Mrs. de Waal who calmed down quickly under the gaze of his stroking, flattering eyes, and the persuasiveness of his voice. When he saw Lizzie his attention was diverted from Mrs. de Waal for just a moment, but not before she had seen his soliciting eyes scanning her figure surreptitiously. She watched him as he walked back to the Mercedes. He had a distinctive walk, light and swift, holding his left hand slightly away from his body, with the little finger separated from the others as if shaking off some unwanted dirt.

Joshua found reason to visit the de Waal household again - "Just a courtesy call Mrs. de Waal, to see if the replacement is to your satisfaction". Lizzie also found a reason to be in the same room. Mrs. de Waal, who was flattered by the extra attention, and pleased with Joshua's manner, introduced him "This is my housekeeper, Lizzie." There was instant chemistry between them.

Lizzie was not yet seventeen when their courtship, her first, started and to her it was very romantic. On their first night out Joshua picked her up in the company car and she watched the lights of the city glimmering on Table Bay as they cruised down de Waal Drive on their way to the cinema. At the interval Joshua bought her a large box of chocolates. She opened it and offered him one. He unwrapped it slowly, put it in his mouth, crushed the paper into a little ball, and then reached for her hand. He put the paper ball into it and then gently closed her hand before he gave it a seductive squeeze. When he kissed her goodnight in the car before she got out at home, Lizzie was in seventh heaven.

That year of their courtship was the most wonderful time in Lizzie's life, their evenings and days out the highlights of her week. Joshua told her about a house in a new development on the Cape Flats that he had his eye on and for which he had been saving up for a while.

He took her to see it on one of their days off; Lizzie thought that life just couldn't get any better.

They were married in the shadow of Table Mountain. Lizzie could think of nothing that could give her more joy than to be the mistress of her own home, and she kept it spotless. Life was good.

The first time Joshua hit her was after a party when they had been married for six months. The following morning, when she stared at her black eyes in the mirror, Joshua came from behind and put his arms around her.

"I'm so sorry my sweetheart, I really am, the drink devil got into me last night. Oh look what I've done!" He stroked the bruises around her eyes gently. "So, so sorry." He kissed the nape of her neck, and stroked her hair. "My beautiful wife what have I been doing to you?" She pulled away but he held her tight. "Liz, please understand man, I wasn't myself! It will never happen again, I promise you."

But it did happen, whenever he was drunk. She thought of leaving him. But where would she go? Home? There was no home. Her parents and younger siblings were still wandering from hovel to hovel, always behind with the rent. She had only to look around her neat little house to know that it would break her heart to give it up. It was all her childhood dreams come true. There must be a way to get Joshua to stop drinking.

Then one evening, when she sat on the veranda waiting for Joshua to come home from work, the thought came to her, that perhaps if she prayed to God to change Joshua back to the man she fell in love with, it might work. When she was a little child her parents sometimes went to the

Apostolic Faith Mission where they sang and clapped their hands, beseeching God to alleviate their plight. He never did. As a child she enjoyed the singing and clapping, and pranced about until she was almost breathless. As she grew older she began to feel that real prayer needed to be done in silence, inside oneself. So it was, that sitting there on the veranda, she prayed silently to God to help Joshua to stop drinking. Afterwards she felt very peaceful inside herself, and when Joshua came home she got up and gave him a kiss. She could smell beer on his breath, but he seemed quite amicable, and they sat down to the meal she had cooked for them. Shortly after that evening she discovered that she was pregnant. When she told Joshua, his eyes went wide as if in wonderment, and then they went very soft. She felt sure that God had answered her prayer because for the first six months of her pregnancy, he didn't hit her once. He kept talking of his little fellow that would soon be there crawling around the floor.

"He'll have fists that'll put everyone into a funk," he would say proudly. "No bastard will scare him!"

She wondered about that, why he saw his little boy as a fighter; not scared of anyone. Was he scared of big heavy fists as a child? She knew so little about his background. He was very reluctant to talk about it - just said that both his parents were dead.

"No brothers or sisters?" she had asked.

"Just a stepbrother."

"Oh. Do you still see him? What's his name?"

"Bester!" He almost spat the name out. "Big fellow, big bloody bully!"

His face had become dark and a little muscle at the corner of his mouth twitched angrily.

She couldn't get anything more out of him. But it made her wonder about the lesions she had noticed all over his body – old scars which he dismissed as 'nothing – just the rough and tumble of boys knocking about.' This kind of anonymous situation suited her. She was not keen to take Joshua to her family. It worked out well that he met them just before the wedding when they all came up to Cape Town, dressed in their very best.

When her belly grew big and she found lovemaking uncomfortable, the softness disappeared from Joshua's eyes. He came home drunk more and more often, but he did not hit her, even though she could see the anger in his eyes. She felt safe. The baby was protecting her, and afterwards, she believed, he would be so proud of his child, that he would never hit her again, and might even stop drinking.

Two weeks before the baby was due, Joshua didn't come home until after midnight. When he did, she could hear by the way he closed the front door that a fury had come in with him, but still she believed she was safe. When he opened the bedroom door the fright came upon her. He had a deep cut above his eye, and there was blood all over his face.

"Joshua! For God's sake man, what have you been doing!"

That was a mistake, she realized later. She should have pretended to be asleep.

"Doing! What have *I* been doing! It's your fault." He pointed to his eye. "This is all your fault!"

His fist landed in her face, and then he grabbed her by the arm and pulled her out of bed. She felt his boot crashing into her belly and the pain shot right up her spine. A merciful blackness descended upon her, and she felt no more pain until she came to in the hospital. There were two faces hovering above her. One she recognized as the midwife who had been visiting her over the months, and the other, a man in a white coat, she assumed was a doctor. His hands were soft when he touched her.

"You've gone into labour Mrs. Aaronson."

He sat down beside her on the bed and worked his fingers across her face. She flinched.

"Yes, a nasty wound. Your husband?"

His eyes said, *I know you didn't fall.*

She nodded.

"He's outside waiting to see you. Do you want him to come in?"

She shook her head. The pain rolled over her, a black mass, everywhere in her body and soul. She held on. Soon she would see her baby.

"It's a little girl!" the midwife announced at last, and then waited for the cry.

It never came.

"Give her the child", the doctor said, and the anger in his voice was palpable.

As she held her stillborn baby in her arms, she felt that something in her had changed forever. She had long ago realized that the God her parents were beseeching didn't exist. Now she knew that the God she had prayed to that night when she sat silently on the veranda didn't exist either. It didn't matter anymore. Nothing mattered anymore. She heard the doctor's voice in the distance.

"Do you want to lay a charge against your husband Mrs. Aaronson?

She felt as if she was coming out of a mist of confusion. Did she have a husband? Then she understood. Joshua.

She shook her head. "I never want to see him again … ever!"

She never knew when and how the fever had set in, it was all a blur. For two weeks she lay in her hospital bed on the edge between life and death. Vaguely she was aware of people coming and going: her mother, looking old and drawn after her long journey to Cape Town; some friends bringing gifts and flowers; and Joshua. He sat silently by her bed, and when she opened her eyes, he started to speak. It was as if the sight of him, and the sound of his voice automatically closed her eyes. It closed more than her eyes. A steel door inside her had shut him out, forever. She was safe behind that door.

When she could leave the hospital, her mother took her home: two rooms for the six of them. Every day she sat out in the sun staring into nothingness. That was all there was, nothingness. Not even her mother's promptings, "Lizzie, you're only nineteen, you can have another baby," could find a chink into the vast emptiness.

But the sun slowly crept into her bones, bringing life into them. It stroked her back, her skin, and the fading scars on her face, until one day she smiled at a butterfly that danced on a stunted buddleia shrub. For the first time she saw how exhausted her mother looked when she came home from cleaning the white peoples' houses. She was an extra mouth to feed on that meagre income. She knew she had to go and earn her own living, but she wondered why she should make that effort to stay alive. Why live at all? Yet death didn't seem an option either. If she had believed in a God and a heaven, she could embrace death to be united with her little girl, but how did she know she wouldn't be cheated out of that one too? It was all an illusion. Life or death, either way it made no difference.

The following morning she washed, made herself neat, and went out to look for work. Outside in the street she turned around and looked at the house she'd just left. She forced the memory of the house where she'd been the mistress, her house, out of her mind and in that instant she knew that she must leave the Cape altogether. Durban would be a good place to go. It was far enough away. She would leave her memories behind, and she would make sure they would not follow her.

In Durban she found it easy to satisfy her employer, Mrs. Evans. Lizzie's experience of housekeeping impressed her, and she was pleased that Lizzie didn't mind doing extra hours when she was organizing a party.

At the end of her first month with the Evans family, Lizzie wrote home, and to placate her guilt of what she had in mind, sent half her wages to her mother. She intended to make this her last communication with them. The past will stay in the past. She wanted nothing or no one to remind her of what had happened, ever.

Her mother wrote back, thanking her profusely for the money, a letter full of gladness over Lizzie's recovery and hoping to hear from her again soon. Lizzie tore the letter up. She had shut her grief and her family out.

When the Evans family planned their holiday in the Berg, they took Lizzie with them to look after the children. As the Drakensberg mountain range came into view, Lizzie grew quiet inside herself. She realized that in Durban she had missed the mountains. As the days passed, something started to open up in her. It was as if the expanse of sky and the majestic mountains had talked to her, soothed her and promised her healing. She knew what she had to do. She gave in her notice to Mrs. Evans.

"But Lizzie, why? Has someone upset you? The children perhaps?

"No Mrs. Evans, you've been good to me. It's the mountain. I've always lived with mountains around me."

"You want to stay on here?"

"Yes Mrs. Evans, I'm sorry."

Mrs. Evans was silent for a while.

"We'll miss you Lizzie, but I understand."

"Thank you Mrs. Evans."

"Have you found work?"

"No, I thought I must tell you first."

Mrs. Evans' pupils grew large. "Oh I see." Lizzie knew she understood. "We're going to visit some friends this afternoon, I'll ask around for you. I'll give you a good reference."

So it was that she came into the de Wit's household. Mrs. de Wit wasn't Mrs. Evans, but Mr. de Wit was kind, and she had a little two-roomed house all to herself. She had the mountain.

Slowly, slowly, as the months went by Lizzie felt the steel door inside her open slightly, and through that opening something poured in. She had no words for it, but it felt benevolent, soft and healing. She thought of her unanswered prayers of the past, prayers that she uttered through need, but this something was coming into her unasked. It was just there.

Then, on a Thursday morning that saw the mountain standing clear and proud against the sky, she walked into the kitchen and found Mr. de Wit standing there with a baby in his arms and an incredible expression of kindness in his eyes.

"Lizzie," his voice was choked, "I found this little mite on the doorstep. Any idea whose baby this could be?"

She took the baby from him, a coloured child, just like her baby, and her heart said: *Yes, it's my baby.*

Mrs. de Wit burst into the kitchen.

"Holy Moses! I thought I heard baby noises. What's going on here?"

"I found it on the doorstep," Mr. de Wit's eyes stroked the little bundle in Lizzie's arms.

Lizzie unwrapped the soft blanket around the naked baby. "It's a little girl", she said, her voice trembling.

Sandra and Bessie stumbled in, wiping the sleep from their eyes.

"Oh look! A baby!" Sandra came up to Lizzie.

Lizzie lowered her arms so that Sandra could see her, and Bessie came to look too.

"Ahhh." Their voices a chorus.

"Whose child is this?" Mrs. de Wit's voice was sharp as she scanned Lizzie's figure, suspicion growing in her eyes, then obviously dismissed the possibility. "Why put it at *our* door?" She looked at her husband, "Who's the father Daniel?"

"How would *I* know that Kate? I'm more interested in who the mother is: she might need help."

Mrs. de Wit snorted. She turned towards Lizzie. "You haven't by any chance seen a pregnant black girl around here, have you Lizzie?"

Lizzie shook her head and faced Daniel de Wit square on.

"Mr. de Wit," her voice was deeply passionate, "the orphanage, they die there sometimes," she swallowed, her eyes pleading. "You are the head of Social Services, it would be easy for you, they will let you adopt her."

Lizzie heard Mrs. de Wit drew breath in shock, and out of her mouth came words she had never thought she'd dare to utter. "People here will admire you and Mrs. de Wit for it, they will think it a very Christian-like thing to do." She saw a fleeting gleam of pride at that prospect in Mrs. de Wit's eye, and took heart. "She *is* nearly white!"

"Yes, but adopt!" Mrs. de Wit's voice was incredulous. "We've got two children of our own, we don't need another."

Lizzie had the strange feeling, as if she were on a stage, had just delivered her bit of the script, and now it was for the other actors to take over.

Daniel stepped forward, closer to Lizzie and the baby. "It's not about our *needs* Kate, it's about the survival of a child."

"Yes, but she's coloured – besides…"

"Kate, most people around here are now trying to live up to the ideal of the rainbow nation. We could…"

"Well let them! Anyway, what's this nonsense about children dying in the orphanage? That's like saying you're not doing your job properly!"

Mr. de Wit shook his head and sighed, as if in despair. "Kate, I don't run the orphanage, I only administer it as a small section of my work. There are many orphans there, many diseases, Aids is rampant, and sometimes they arrive half starved already." A plaintive sound came from the little bundle in Lizzie's arms. "God Kate – we've got *so* much!" He swallowed as he looked at the baby trying to wriggle her tiny hands from the blanket. "What I was going to say when you interrupted me…" he paused for a moment, "we don't need to actually adopt her, we could just foster her."

"Foster her? What exactly would that entail?"

"In this case, it would mean that she would be fed, clothed, and cared for. In short she would survive."

"Oh please Mummy, she's so cute!" Sandra's bright blue eyes were begging.

"Yes please!" Bessie was jumping up and down with excitement.

"It's all very well trying to make me feel guilty with stories of starvation in orphanages Daniel, and you two," she gestured to the children, "you just think it is a doll to play with. Who do you think is going to look after it at night when it cries?"

Lizzie knew it was her turn on the script. She didn't hesitate.

"*I* will Mrs. de Wit, she won't give you any trouble - I'll take care of her."

"You Lizzie? Living with you?"

Lizzie nodded vigorously. She saw a shrewd, calculating expression on Mrs. de Wit's face.

"I guess you could teach her how to do the housework. When she's bigger she could help around the house. Well, let's think about it"

That day was a turning point in Lizzie's life. When Mr. and Mrs. de Wit were arguing whether to keep the child or take her to the orphanage, her first impulse was to beseech God to let them keep the baby, her baby. It was her deepest need, her deepest desire, but there was no God. Her prayers, and her parent's prayers had never been answered. She was standing there with the baby in her arms, shaking slightly, looking from husband to wife, from wife to husband. Who would win?

It was then that she became aware of that benevolent Presence flowing gently into her heart. Her body became very still. *I will ask it*, she said to herself. '*It will help me; I know that.* It was a wordless prayer, a mere alignment between her and...what? She did not know.

But that evening when she lay in her bed with an incredible sense of gratitude, it struck her that she had

31

actually prayed, and that her prayer *had* been answered. She could feel the Presence – it was there, with her, and she addressed it.

Who are you, she asked in her mind, *are you God?*

Her heart answered: *I am you, or the mountain, or the light in the sky, the birds, or God. I am all that is.*

With her hands folded across her heart, Lizzie fell into a deep dreamless sleep until the cries of a baby woke her. She was on her feet in an instant.

So Lizzie's new life started, revolving around Miriam. In the mornings she would wheel her into the big house where Sandra and Bessie would coo over her, and even Mrs. de Wit would have baby talk with her. "She's a lovely little thing," she would say afterwards to Sandra and Bessie. "Now you two, go get yourselves ready for school."

Lizzie was happy. She went about her duties with swift hands and feet, and her heart was singing. The days passed. The months passed. The years passed, each marking something new: Miriam crawling, Miriam walking, first with unsteady legs falling over, getting up and walking again, Miriam talking, little words uttered with glee, then little sentences accompanied by gestures. Lizzie saw the child's bright eyes following first the pictures, then the letters, as at night, she read her stories from Sandra and Bessie's old baby books.

When Miriam was four she haltingly read the stories out loud to herself, and by the age of five she read them fluently to Lizzie. From a few planks they hammered a small bookcase together and for her sixth birthday, Lizzie bought her a thick volume of children's classics which, together, they pored over when she wasn't teaching her how to clean and cook and iron. Her life had meaning.

And now they were going to take Miriam away from her. Where was that Presence now? Could it not have prevented this? Had that been an illusion too? Intuitively she knew that if she lost faith in its existence, she would descend into an indescribable darkness. Yet all through her duties performed with swift hands, it was starting to slip away, slip away....

That night their two-roomed house sheltered her and Miriam from the unstoppable rain, but not from their despair. Their dinner remained on the table untouched. They had no appetite. Lizzie stood staring out of the window as the mountain faded away in the darkness, taking with it her flimsy, impossible plans of fleeing with Miriam before they could hand her over to Mr. Mynhard. Her thoughts were very bitter. No matter that there was no longer apartheid. The whites still have the power. She brought Miriam up, yet no one even bothered to consult her. It was as if, to them, she had no feelings. Miriam had no feelings! Her eyes narrowed and her lips became a thin line as her thoughts raced through her head in angry swirls: *these white people! They have 'us' and 'them,' ingrained into their brains! Even now they can't see we are humans too.*

She thought of Mr. de Wit and her mouth relaxed slightly as if some inner part of her was putting a case forward in their defence; but she would not budge. Even a kind-hearted person like Mr. de Wit... That argument of his: *Doing our bit to create a rainbow nation* - just some veneer, that was all it was, Lizzie thought, grief washing over her. Just putting on a show of being open-minded and kind to these poor people. Even Sandra and Bessie, they didn't seem too bothered about Miriam going either. It was great playing with her when she was a baby, a toddler, but they never cared to get close to her. She was after all just a coloured child that their parents had done a favour, and she, Lizzie, was powerless to do anything about it. Powerless and poor – *that* was it: poverty. If you had money and education, no matter your skin colour, you had power.

"I don't want to leave you Aunty Lizzie." Miriam's voice penetrated her musings, sounding thin and forlorn. Lizzie turned away from the window.

"I'll come and see you as often as I can," she said, conjuring up ways and means in her mind of how to cross the forty odd miles that would separate them.

"Will I still see the mountain from Mr Bruno's house?" The anxiety in Miriam's eyes cut through Lizzie.

"Yes, but from the other side,"

"And God, will I still see God?"

Lizzie shook her head. "No Miriam, you can only see him from this side."

Miriam's words were just audible through her sobs. "I'm going to lose both my father and mother. How can God do this to me?"

It was as if Miriam's words had galvanized Lizzie into some power beyond her own capabilities. She stopped herself from slipping into darkness. She could not let Miriam descend into despair. How would a child cope with that? She put her arm around Miriam's shoulders.

"Miriam, listen. Do you remember that magician who came to your school last year?"

Miriam nodded her head while trying to wipe her nose.

"Well, God is a bit like a magician." Lizzie wiped Miriam's tears away. "He can be on the mountain and at the same time he can live in your heart."

"He can live in my heart? My heart is not big enough!"

"Miriam, a magician can do anything, he can make himself big and tall like a rock, or make himself into a single ray of light that can easily slip into your heart, and live there always. Just think of it, then you will never be away from God, he will be there straight away when you want to talk to him, or ask for help."

Lizzie saw Miriam grow calmer.

"Is that true Aunty Lizzie?"

"Have I ever told you a lie, my love?"

Miriam shook her head.

"Well then, I'm telling you, God will leave here with you, he will ride in your heart, and will live there forever."

"But he will also stay on the mountain won't he Aunty Lizzie, so that he can look after you?"

Lizzie clasped the child to her heart, rocking them both to and fro, nodding her head, while the tears streamed down her face.

That night Miriam did not sleep in her own bed, she crawled into Aunty Lizzie's as she had done when she was little and had woken up frightened at night. Several times she was on the verge of telling Aunty Lizzie about the strange voice that had come into her head, but something stopped her. There was a vague knowing in her that she could not form into words. This voice was something sacred, something so close to her, so entwined within her being, that talking about it now would be like clipping the wings of a bird.

In the early morning hours, just before daybreak, she dreamed of a white eagle swooping low over the valley screeching, searching the low cliffs near the big houses before it soared up into a deep blue sky, disappearing behind the mountain.

The Saturday morning of the departure dawned bright and clear. By 9 o'clock Daniel de Wit had brought the car out of the garage and the boot stood open, ready to receive Miriam's suitcase. Lizzie was carrying it, holding Miriam by the arm with her free hand as if scared that the frightened child might take flight and disappear down into the valley. For a moment she thought that it was actually going to happen when Miriam suddenly held back and stopped. Following her gaze up to the mountain, Lizzie saw a small drifting cloud that had attached itself to one side of the upright rock, Miriam's God, like an outstretched arm reaching out to her.

Lizzie detached herself from Miriam and walked quickly to the car in an effort to hold back her tears, but not before she had seen Miriam saluting the mountain. Daniel de Wit took the suitcase from Lizzie and glanced at Miriam, then quickly cast his eyes down as if he had been intruding on sacred ground. Lizzie had seen that expression of reverence on his face before, when he was watching Miriam, one year old, crawling around the garden. Black frizzy curls lifted by the breeze as she pulled herself up on the garden furniture, sparkling green eyes, and that joyful laugh which came with that first feat of putting one foot before the other without holding on. Lizzie slammed the car boot closed just as Kate de Wit came out of the house, her tight skirt threatening to ride up above her knee.

"All ready then Miriam?"

She didn't wait for an answer.

"Lizzie, please make sure Bessie doesn't sleep 'til mid day again, she's playing tennis with Dr. Evans' son at two o'clock."

She opened the front door and swung her shapely legs across the car seat. Lizzie saw the car pulling away, the two grown-ups in the front and the child, all alone in the back, sitting stiffly staring at the mountain. Then Miriam turned and waved to Lizzie: a frantic little hand trying to hide the pleading eyes.

Lizzie knew she was going to be sick and rushed towards the prefab house, a house that now seemed large and empty, as if it had lost its soul.

Chapter 3

When they arrived at Mr. Bruno's house a shroud of mist was covering his side of the mountain, but it didn't matter, because Miriam knew God wouldn't be there anyway. She remembered what Aunty Lizzie had said about God travelling with her in her heart, but she couldn't see that light that he was supposed to be. There was just a dull and dark thudding inside her. All she could think of was that long frown on Mr. Bruno's face and head, and she didn't dare think of her school and Miss Lang's smile, or else she would cry, and Mrs. de Wit got annoyed when people cried, and Mr. de Wit's eyes would go very sad, and she didn't want to make him sad.

Mr. Bruno came out onto the veranda in his electric wheelchair to meet them, and the two big dogs following him wagged their tails. He looked pale, and it was while he was greeting Mr. and Mrs. de Wit that she saw the hand that had gone lame. It sat on his lap like a lump of meat. She stared at it and then felt a strange thing happening in her heart, but before she could figure it out, it was her turn to greet Mr. Bruno.

"That your luggage Miriam?" he was pointing to her suitcase, which a man he called Filamon, was lifting from the boot.

"Yes Mr. Bruno."

He smiled with only half his frown showing, and she felt a little bit less scared.

"Got any treasures in there?"

He was sounding like her schoolmates now, and without thinking she said:

"Yes Mr. Bruno."

He lifted his eyebrows and said, "Oh?"

She knew she was trapped, and started kicking the small stones in front of her around, looking at the ground.

"A secret, is it?"

Mr. de Wit chuckled and hearing that made her feel better. When she lifted her eyes she saw Mrs. de Wit's tight skirt disappearing into the house, but she also saw the lame hand on Mr. Bruno's lap again, and that funny feeling came back into her heart. That was when she said:

"It's my pictures Mr. Bruno, the ones I painted at school. Miss Lang said I could take them with me."

"Pictures! You paint pictures!"

"Yes Mr. Bruno."

"Well, well, you must be even cleverer than I thought."

She could feel the blood rushing to her cheeks and was glad when Mrs. De Wit shouted from the house.

"Come on in Miriam!"

She ran to the front door.

Mrs. de Wit was waiting. "I'll show you your room", she said.

Miriam felt scared again. Her room? She got to sleep in a room all by herself? Her heart was aching for Aunty Lizzie, and that kind of feeling she knew very well.

She walked in behind Mrs. de Wit, and at a glance she could see almost the whole house: the lounge, dining room, and the kitchen, all had a place in this large room. Not a bit like Mr. and Mrs. de Wit's house. Then she understood: Mr. Bruno could run around it in his wheelchair easily with no doors and walls to bother him. In front of the stove a thickset, very dark skinned woman was cooking something that smelled kind of sour. She greeted Mrs. de Wit in the Zulu language and didn't look at Miriam until Mrs. de Wit said:

"Katrina, this is Miriam."

"Eh he, dumella.*" She scanned Miriam's skin and hair the way people who were either white or black always looked at her. Then she cast her eyes down again, and Miriam couldn't make out whether Katrina liked her or not, and she didn't know whether she liked Katrina or not.

She followed Mrs. de Wit down the wide corridor.

---

* a greeting.

"This is Mr. Mynhard's room. This is the spare room, and this one opposite Mr. Mynhard's room is where you will sleep so that you can hear him if he needs you at night."

Miriam's throat went tight, and she couldn't say 'Yes, Mrs. de Wit'. But Mrs. de Wit wouldn't have heard her in any case because she was already marching towards the kitchen where she ordered Katrina to make tea, "And bring some biscuits in as well."

Back in the living area, and coming into it from the bedrooms, Miriam noticed on the wall in the dining section a very large bookcase. It was filled with books, roads maps, atlases, and a built in computer desk. Her curiosity was aroused, she had never seen so many books in a person's house, and she stopped in front of them, looking at everything with interest. She didn't realize that Mrs. de Wit was right behind her.

"Lucky devil," she said, as if talking to herself, "he can get broadband here; not like us, still stuck with only the telephone. But he might just as well not have it," her sharp voice sounded bitter, "all he seems to use it for is Internet banking, and the odd order from the shops."

Miriam had never worked on a computer, but she knew what it looked like. She had seen it in the library in town a few times when Mr. de Wit took her with him to go and fetch Sandra and Bessie when they did their assignments there.

Katrina was carrying the tea tray out onto the veranda and Miriam and Mrs. de Wit followed. They heard Mr. de Wit say: "Yes, it was a frightful storm, like war had broken out. Glad it wasn't so bad here or you might have feared for the erosion of your dirt track."

"Oh yes, that awful road," Mrs. de Wit interrupted. "When are you going to have it tarred? Widened, so that big delivery trucks can come in, and people can turn round in it." Mrs. de Wit sounded quite irritated.

"I'm not catering for other people Kate." Mr. Bruno's long frown was back. "We're almost self sufficient here.

The few things I need from the shops can be delivered by small vehicles."

"You've become a real recluse these days!"

"Kate!" Mr. de Wit held his hand up. "Lay off now, please."

Mrs. de Wit pouted and started on her tea and biscuits.

Mr. Bruno called into the house and Katrina appeared. He spoke to her in Zulu and then said to Miriam: "Go with Katrina, she'll show you the outbuildings and what they're used for."

Miriam quickly swallowed her tea and got up, glancing at the plate of biscuits.

"Take a couple with you Miriam," Mr. de Wit said, smiling softly at her.

She took two and saw Mr. Bruno's frown from the corner of her eye. She wished that Mr. de Wit wasn't going to leave soon.

Katrina led her around the house, and not too far from the back door she saw a long low building with two separate doors leading into it. Katrina opened the first, "for washing," she said. Miriam saw a washing machine, ironing board and neat cupboards lining one wall. It was a bright room, looking out onto the shrouded mountain. The next room was less neat. It had boxes piled up in one corner and a couple of fold up beds stacked up in another. There were other bits and pieces lying around.

"Sometimes to sleep," Katrina said, and Miriam assumed it was some kind of a spare room – seldom used.

Outside Katrina lead the way, waddling down a slight slope, past the chicken coop where cackling hens surveyed them with beady eyes. A smell of chicken manure drifted towards them on the light breeze. They came to a vegetable garden where the man who carried her suitcase in, and whom Mr. Bruno called Filamon, stood bent over, weeding. He straightened up as they approached and saluted Miriam.

"Yebo!"

In Filamon's shining dark eyes, his wide, white-teeth smile was clearly reflected, and she thought the contrast with his black skin lovely.

"Good morning," she said and felt herself relaxing slightly as his friendliness washed over her.

Katrina and Fillamon talked for a while in Zulu before she took her back home and into the kitchen where she showed her inside the cupboards.   The crockery and cutlery were neatly housed, everything in its appointed place.   The atmosphere felt unfriendly to Miriam, heavy, and her heart sank.

When she got back to the veranda Mr. and Mrs. de Wit were about to leave. It had started raining and Miriam swallowed hard to hold back the tears that threatened to spill out. She felt as if she was standing all-alone in a vast desert, with nothing around her but fear.

It rained for the rest of the day and in the night Miriam heard the plop, plop of the drops on the roof, until she didn't hear anything any more.

When she woke the sun was bright on her bedroom window. She slipped into some clothes and went outside to see what the mountain looked like on Mr. Bruno's side. She thought it was very beautiful too. Reaching for the sky, it's high peaks and tooth-like rocks here and there made her think of the smiling photo of her that Mr. de Wit took when she was changing teeth. A sweet smell wafted on the wind, and she looked around to see where it came from.   There were azaleas planted all around the edge of the garden, as if protecting the house, but the smell came from the honeysuckle creeping stealthily along the fence. It was when she turned around to look at the veranda that she saw it.

The Hand.

There it sat on the long table: slightly bigger than life size, strong and muscular carved out of marble, looking as though it could be begging. A few scattered raindrops were still glittering in its palm.   She wondered that she hadn't seen it when she arrived, but then this was a new day, bright and sunny, while yesterday was misty, and inside her it was aching so much. She crept nearer and touched it. It felt smooth and her fingers slid effortlessly along its contours as if something magical in it was guiding her movements. She loved it, the beauty of it, the feel of it, and she kept stroking, imagining that they were holding hands, the two of them. It was a comforting thought. She thought of Mr. Bruno's lame hand and the contrast couldn't have been greater. Then she understood what was happening in her heart when she first saw it: a deep sense of kindness, of wanting to make it better.

High up in the sky she heard a screeching sound, and turned around to look. There, as if flying straight out of the mountain was an enormous white eagle; like the one in her dream. The shivers ran down her spine as she watched it swoop low, then rise up into the air, and lifted itself above the mountain before flying away.

She felt less scared and lonely as if she had made two friends: a hand to hold hers and an eagle to lift her gaze towards the wide horizon.

On Mr. Bruno's side of the mountain life settled down to its lonely pace. On weekday mornings Miriam had lessons from the ex-school master. She soon learned that routine was all-important to him. Lunch had to be served exactly at one, and Katrina knew that, knew exactly how to cook his food, how to serve it, and when the dishes had to be done so that there would be no noise when he went for his afternoon nap.

The lessons took the same form. No subject was to encroach on the time of another. Miriam found that rigid routine very hard, especially in the art lesson. She loved the large sheets of paper Mr. Bruno would have her spread out on the table on the veranda, and the paint and brushes that she could choose from. She painted the garden with the azaleas, and Mr. Bruno nodded his approval. She wanted to do more; the mountain and the clouds, but the time was up and Mr. Bruno told her to pack up and go and wash her hands for lunch.

"Oh Mr. Bruno, can't I go on? I'm not hungry, really Mr. Bruno."

He shook his head but his eyes had a friendly gleam to them.

"No, we have to have our meals at regular times."

"After lunch Mr. Bruno?"

"After lunch to-day I want you to help Katrina with the ironing. Bit by bit I want her to show you exactly how I want things done here. How I want my shirts folded and exactly where to put them. This Saturday I want her to show you how to cook my vegetables. You see on her off days you will have to do the cooking, which I was told you could do very well. OK?"

Miriam swallowed hard at the tightness in her throat – the anger that wanted to jump out. Wanted to shout: *No! I want to paint!* But inside her the threat of the orphanage stood on guard, like a shadowy soldier.

"Yes Mr. Bruno," she said.

They ate their meal in silence. Mr. Bruno chewed his food thoroughly and she knew he would finish exactly at 1.30, and that she would be expected to do the same. After lunch Mr. Bruno got into his buggy and went outside to see if Filamon had tended the vegetable garden, and she knew he would inspect the hen pen too. In the meantime Katrina quickly cleared the table and did the dishes. When he came back it was time to go and rest, and Miriam was told to do the same.

"You've worked hard at your lessons Miriam. At your age you need to rest before your afternoon duties."

Miriam lay on her bed, bored, longing to be outside in the sunshine, longing for her old school playmates, wondering what Sandra and Bessie were doing now, deeply longing for Aunty Lizzie. She felt desperate and started crying, burying her face in the pillow so that Mr. Bruno would not hear her.

The screeching reached her ears as her shoulders were shaking and she stopped her sobs. The eagle. Her eagle! Silently she slipped off her bed and pressed her face against the window. She could see its white body sailing away in the sky, and her heart melted inside her. One of her new found friends! Did it come to console her? She crept back to her bed and gave herself over to the sleep that enfolded her, like the arms of a mother.

She was woken by the hissing of Mr. Bruno's wheelchair and knew it was time for the afternoon routine.

"Take the dogs for a walk Miriam, they need exercise, and so do you. Mind you don't get them excited!"

Miriam was pleased that this task, which had been Filamon's, had now been handed over to her. They walked down the azalea-lined driveway, and the dogs, as if in anticipation of time out from their usual controlled obedience, strained at their leashes, panting in the spring sunshine. Soon the driveway opened up to the dirt track, and she let them run free. They went wild with delight, and Cinnamon, the slender one, galloped into the long grass like a gazelle, her fawn coat blending into it. Honey plodded along close to Miriam, in the hope of a cuddle before she set off to sniff out lizards and insects.

Where the road made a fork, a rock with a flat top had settled itself into the field and Miriam decided to climb onto it. The dogs joined her and sniffed around a bit before they made off again, joyously, free! She sat down on the warm stone scanning the azure above her. The breeze of the morning had quieted down, and the air was like someone holding their breath. Miriam sat transfixed, looking from mountain to sky, from sky to mountain, until they became one, releasing a white eagle which, for a moment, hung motionless in the still air. Then it sailed away in majestic splendour.

The two images were ingrained in Miriam's brain, and she knew she would paint them. Yet her eagle, hanging in its perfect stillness, would not be for Mr. Bruno's eyes.

The companionship and comfort it brought to her would be her secret.

She pulled her knees up and put her head on her arms. She felt light headed and swayed slightly from side to side. It felt as if something in her head had opened up, expanded to embrace the sky, the mountain, the eagle and the veld with all the creatures living in it. She had a deep sense of an all-pervading peace bestowed upon her like a gift – a treasure. For her, foundling Miriam.

As the months went by Bruno became more and more intrigued with the watercolours and acrylics Miriam was doing in the art lessons. There was one picture that especially fascinated him: a mountain and sky melting into each other. When he gazed at it he felt transported above his lame limbs into something he was, or should be, or would be. But he could not pin words to it.

One day when he was out in the garden inspecting Filamon's work, he saw the corner of a paper sticking out from underneath an azalea bush, and immediately he steered his wheelchair in that direction. He felt annoyed that Filamon had left rubbish lying around. With his stick he poked at it, slid it closer to him, and then picked it up with his helping hand. It was a white sheet of paper encased in a thick, waterproof plastic sheath. He turned it over. A magnificent white eagle spread its wings from side to side across the paper, as if the whole universe was its domain. He stared, the shivers running through his spine. He felt joy, the first in many, many years. It was akin to the exhilaration he felt when Amelie was born and she closed her little hand around his finger. Then sadness overcame him, and the pain of Amelie's death surfaced acutely. Suddenly he felt angry with Miriam. So, she's been painting secretly! Breaking his rules, breaking the routine!

"Filamon!" he shouted. "Filamon, come here!"

Down at the bottom of the vegetable patch, Filamon stuck the spade calmly in the soil and walked up the path with rhythmic movements, his strong lean body gleaming in the sunshine. He stood before Bruno.

"Yebo Master." He gave a mock salute in response to Bruno's rude summoning, and Bruno, picking up on it, felt slightly ridiculous.

"Where is Miriam?" His voice had lost its commanding tone.

Filamon shrugged his shoulders. "Perhaps walking with the dogs." .

So that was it then, that was when she made her secret sketches!

"O.K. Filamon", and as Filamon turned to leave, "thank you."

Filamon left with a faint smile hovering between amusement and compassion.

Bruno was puzzled. Why did she hide it in the garden? Did she think he would snoop around her room while she was out? He looked at the eagle again and intuitively understood why Miriam had kept it a secret. It was sacred to her. Private, like his own thoughts.

That was one of the main bones of contention between him and Valerie he thought: she wanted to know all the ins and outs of their children's lives, all their secrets. He frowned upon it, protested. It always sparked a quarrel.

"Just because you're so tight arsed doesn't mean our children have to be the same!"

Her shrill voice irritated him and he frowned. "They have the right to their privacy, you shouldn't go snooping into their bedside lockers!"

"Yeah, and I guess you have the right to those brooding thoughts of yours, making your face look like midnight even on the brightest day. You never share your thoughts, your feelings!" She was standing in front of him hands on hips, a sensual stance, and despite his anger he could feel desire stirring in him. She was quite a bit younger than him - he was already thirty-five when they got married - and still a very attractive women.

He kept his anger under control during those quarrels, and often they ended in sexual intimacy. But after Amelie's death something snapped in him, and the anger rose up out of its coffin like a ghost undeterred by nails, tight screws, and six feet of soil.

The first time he hit Valerie was when he found her furtively reading Ben's letters which were tucked away under a sheet of paper at the bottom of his locker drawer. It was just one swipe, which knocked her sideways. They didn't speak to each other for days after that, and even when they were on speaking terms again, it was only about practical matters. Then one day he found her rummaging through the box where he kept all the little cards Amelie had made for him at school. He had tied them up with ribbons in date order, and had put the box at the back in his desk drawer. He saw red and could not stop himself. Valerie's face was black and blue and one eye was swollen. She had a broken arm. When the fury had subsided, he stood helpless before the image of his father, his violent father, mocking him from beyond the grave. He apologised profusely, promised her it would never ever happen again, but it was too late. There was too little left between them to survive that attack. Of course, in a divorce court, if the facts were known, he would stand no chance of custody for Ben. In fact, he might have difficulty in gaining visiting rights. He could not face it if it were to be known at school, where both he and Valerie were teaching. He might even lose his job. Luckily Valerie didn't want that either, she wanted him out of her life, but she wanted maintenance for Ben. She stated her ultimatum:

"You get the hell out of this district, pay me maintenance for Ben, and finance his university education when the time comes. I'll give out that I had *fallen* down the stairs."

He had lost both his children.

In his new post in Cape Town he made one very firm resolution: he would stay calm and in control of himself, no matter what. He succeeded. He threw himself into the life of the school. His hard work and dedication stood him in good stead when he applied for the headmaster's post when it came available. Everything was going well. Everything was under control.

Except his limbs.

He became aware that his legs were not as strong as they used to be. He used to be able to cycle for a good stretch of miles, but now they seemed to be getting weaker and weaker. There was an intermittent tingling sensation, which was getting stronger and stronger on every return. He found himself limping, and the limp was getting more and more noticeable. He went to see his doctor and they started exploratory tests.

He was allowed to see Ben once a month, and conscientiously he made the trip to the West Cape, but Ben never seemed really pleased to see him. He sensed so much anger in the boy that it scared him.

He would take him out to a restaurant. "We'll go to the Spur," he would say.

Ben would pull a face as if he was going to be sick. "Yuck, they don't have real food there. I want to go to MacDonald's."

"The Spur has good healthy food, salads and vegetables and fresh fruit, and you can help yourself to as much as you like." He had his schoolmaster's voice on.

"Ha, ha, who wants to heap their plate with that stuff?"

"Well Ben, that's where we're going. I'm not going to let you eat rubbish."

Ben's voice rung high with defiance "You can't stop me eating what I want when I'm with my mother!"

What would his father have done to him if he had said that!! Well, he wasn't his father - a violent man. So he kept quiet, yet marched Ben to the Spur, where they ate their food in a gloomy silence. Going to meet with Ben was eroding his defences.

When the test results were available the doctor called him in. He sounded apologetic.

"I'm afraid it points to muscular dystrophy. There are many types of muscle-wasting conditions, each affecting different muscles. We're not sure what causes it – often it is hereditary, but sometimes it can just occur out of the blue." He scanned his notes. "You said you're not aware that anyone in your family suffered from it, didn't you?"

Bruno nodded and shifted nervously on his chair. "Are there any drugs available for it? Or are there... I mean what else can be done for it?"

The doctor looked down on the report in front of him. "There are some drugs we can try – but it will all depend on how well you can tolerate the side effects. We have no sure cure for it. As I said, we don't know what causes it, but our experience is that most conditions are progressive with the muscles gradually weakening over time. The one consolation is that, usually, there is no pain."

Bruno could hear the wind blowing through the trees outside, a howling sound - like a lone jackal crying out to the night. The doctor was silent for a moment, then moved his bifocals down his nose and looked at Bruno over the rim.

"Bruno, I am a man of science and am greatly respectful of scientific discoveries, but science does not have all the answers. There are other things that *I* suspect can play a big role in the onset and prognosis of a disease ... like feelings, beliefs, guilt, and," he hesitated, "grief." He pushed his glasses back on his nose and looked down on his prescription pad. "For that I do not have a cure. We can transplant a *faulty* heart, but as yet we can't mend a broken one." He got up. "Physiotherapy, hydrotherapy and diet all could play a useful part, and perhaps you could arrange that Ben visited you, rather than you him. It's a long trip and exhausting for you"

Ben seldom came. There was always an excuse: too much homework, a rugby match, a party at a friend's, always something that could not be missed.

Bruno got started on the drugs and religiously took his medication, closely watching out for any improvements. But his muscles stayed weak, and were getting weaker, even though he had incorporated physiotherapy. Worst of all was the foggy feeling it caused in his head – he struggled to think clearly and was often unfocussed, muddling information up. It was when he had an alarming experience of feeling totally disorientated when he was addressing his staff that he decided: *that was it! He was giving the drug treatment up.*

He continued with his physiotherapy, but somehow, for him, there remained a vague association between it and the drugs. He extended it to hydrotherapy. It was easier, and more relaxing doing the exercises in the warm water but his heart was not in it.

With his mind cleared from the effects of the drugs he read up on nutrition: modern theories, as well as ancient Indian and Chinese methods of food combinations and found it very interesting. It felt to him that the correct diet could be of benefit to him. He consulted a nutritionist with knowledge of a wide range of different methods of healing through what we eat, and she prescribed a dietary regime for his specific ailment. She convinced him that the way the food was prepared and eaten was important. He employed a coloured girl to come in and cook for him the way it was prescribed - buying ready meals was out now! He ate in silence, fully focussed on each mouthful and the good he felt it would do to his body. After a month he was certain that his digestion had improved and that therefore the nutrients were now more available to his muscles.

However by the time Ben matriculated Bruno's mobility had deteriorated to walking with a stick and he had given up on the physiotherapy and hydrotherapy. It was just too time consuming. Ben came to visit and to discuss funding for his university degree for which Bruno had set the money aside. Ben was no longer the obnoxious schoolboy, and they didn't argue. Bruno was proud to pay for his son's education.

"You're a bright young man Ben," he had said. "What are you planning to read at uni?"

"Psychology Dad."

"Psychology! Well, I thought you might rather go for one of the sciences, become a scientific researcher or something.

"Psychology *is* a science in its own right Dad, and much research has been, and can be done. I intend to specialize in Industrial Psychology later."

There was an edge to Ben's voice, which reminded Bruno of the Spur versus MacDonald's arguments. It was a controlled edge. Bruno wasn't going to test the strength of that control; but he was deeply disappointed, even resentful: psychology – endlessly analysing people's feelings and motives, just like Valerie did, always insisting that he spill his guts. And that he had to pay for *that.*

By the time Ben sat his finals, Bruno, and the school board, knew early retirement was on the cards. His energy had dropped to a very low level. Just getting himself ready for school in the morning exhausted him. The impending loss of his position as headmaster, of work, weakened his legs even more. Trying to hold the use of a wheelchair at bay was no longer an option. It was then that Daniel came up with the idea:

"Why don't you move up to the Berg, Bruno? Then you can put the Cape behind you. And you'll be near us. Kate and the girls are very fond of you, you know."

"But I would like to still take an interest in the school, perhaps serve on the school board or something."

Daniel had touched his arm in that warm way of his.

"It's up to you Bruno, of course, but it could be very painful, such a long lingering letting go. A clean break might be easier."

Daniel was right of course. He felt so much criticism and just couldn't see eye to eye with the new headmaster. It wasn't just over school matters: the mere mention of the controversy going on in the newspapers between the so called 'open minded' and 'narrow minded' people, about the pending ending of apartheid, was enough to spark palpable tension between them. And Bruno wasn't shy to state his conviction – and to state it forcefully.

"It is inevitable man! Can't you see that? We don't want a bloodbath! We should go with it, it's the only way forward!"

They could very quickly get into deep emotional waters.

He knew he had to cut with the Cape and with his past there; his health was deteriorating. The tingling in his arm had started.

After he had settled into the smallholding, the tingling in his arm subsided. That was a consolation. His legs seemed stronger too. Life was very tranquil in the Berg, even when apartheid did end it hardly affected him. It was like watching it from a distance sitting in his crime free sphere.

He briefly considered going down to attend Ben's graduation ceremony. It was Daniel, again, that laid the facts bare for him:

"Valerie and her husband will be there, and perhaps their daughter too. The emotional strain might set you back again Bruno, and you have just picked up so well."

This time he accepted Daniel's advice without arguing. After all, it wasn't as if Ben was receiving a worthwhile degree. Psychology! Imagine! Even if the boy had read literature as he had done, it would have meant something. That could have led to a teaching post – even a headmaster's post eventually.

Bruno was shaken out of his reverie when from down the road he heard Miriam whistling to the dogs. Quickly he put the sketch in his hand back in its plastic sheath and placed it under the bush where he had found it. He turned his wheelchair around and went to his room. He sat at the window and watched the garden from behind the net curtains. Miriam made little playful runs with the dogs, then stopped to fondle their ears. When she was near the row of azalea bushes, she scanned the veranda, the garden and the vegetable patch. She made a quick dash for that bush, and retrieved the picture. It disappeared under her sweater like lightning. So that's how it is, Bruno thought; she hides it while she's out, then takes it to her room when she's back.

That evening over dinner he looked at Miriam with new eyes. She was beginning to fill out. Not quite breasts yet, but a body that was preparing itself to take a leap into a new dimension. Now he was glad that Lizzie came to visit once a month. To begin with he felt irritated by the disruption to his routine, but now he realized that the guidance of a woman was necessary for her. He cleared his throat.

"Miriam, can you ride a bicycle?"

"Oh yes Mr. Bruno, I was allowed to learn on Bessie's bike. Aunty Lizzie taught me."

"Good. And can you ride a bicycle with a shopping basket on the back, and one on the handles?"

"I can try Mr. Bruno, I can learn. Why?"

"Well, I thought perhaps you could fetch some vegetables from the farm stalls sometimes instead of me getting it delivered."

"Oh yes Mr. Bruno, I can even ride into town for you!"

"Five miles is a bit far for now I think. Perhaps later when you are a bit bigger and stronger."

"Sure Mr. Bruno."

The green eyes sparkled in the bronze skin, and Bruno's eyes followed the fall of the frizzy curls around her face. She should paint a self-portrait, he thought. Perhaps he should put her in front of a mirror with paint and brushes.

Later that evening it was time for Miriam's routine: to lock up and check all the windows; put Bruno's hot water bottle in his bed exactly at the right spot where his feet would be; draw his curtains and put his urinal, which lived inside the bedside cupboard during the day, on top of it within easy reach for him during the night. Bruno didn't feel like going to bed but he forced himself. Late nights would just set him back again, he thought. He needed a regular life.

He fell into a fitful sleep, awakening every couple of hours. It was towards the early hours of the morning when he went into a deep sleep, that he had the dream: he was engulfed in a dark cloud from which there seemed no escape. He felt desperately unhappy, and from that too there was no escape. Then, as he watched, the cloud started to tremble around him as a ray of brilliant bright light pierced through it and went straight for his heart. He put his hand on his heart as if to protect it, and the light withdrew, hovering at the edge of the cloud. It was as if it was waiting. After a while it dimmed and disappeared, and the darkness descended upon him again. He screamed: 'No! No!' and thrashed about with his good arm until he woke up.

Miriam was standing in the doorway, and the dogs were barking.

"Did you call me Mr. Bruno?"

He looked at the girl in her white night dress, and in his sleep fogged mind, she looked like an angel came to rescue him.

He shouted: "Yes please! Please!" Then his mind cleared and he saw Miriam looking at him wide eyed. The dogs were now barking nervously.

"No, sorry Miriam, it was a bad dream. Go calm the dogs down and go back to bed."

"Yes Mr. Bruno." She disappeared from his sight: a bit like the light, he thought, as he reached for the glass of water on his bedside table.

The following morning his legs felt weak and he had difficulty in getting up. At about eleven o'clock the phone rang. That annoyed Bruno. *Who can be so inconsiderate,* he thought? *Everyone in the Berg knows I teach in the morning. They also know when I eat and when I rest. People know I don't like to be disturbed during those times. It must be urgent.*

He swung his wheelchair around and went to answer the phone.

"Dad, how are you?"

Bruno held his annoyance in tightly.

"Fine Ben, just in the middle of teaching."

There was a moment of confused silence on the other end of the line, then:

"Oh yes, the foundling. Sorry Dad, I'd forgotten."

For some reason Bruno felt offended by this remark, but before he could retort, Ben went on.

"Listen Dad, I'd like to come and see you. I'm having a week's holiday in Durban and thought I'd come up to the Berg."

"Fine, when will you set off?"

"Just after lunch, should be with you around 4 o'clock."

When Bruno returned to his school table where Miriam was engrossed in studying a map of South America, his hand was shaking and his thoughts were racing trying to figure out how long ago it was since Ben last visited: *must have been at least two years ago, may be even more, and then he was full of the promotion at the so called Psychology Research Institute in Cape Town that he had just been given. As if it wasn't about time too at the age of thirty two.*

He clenched his teeth, his afternoon and evening routine was going to be disrupted and he felt totally out of sorts.

Chapter 4

Miriam took the dogs for their walk. She had started a new game with them: throwing a ball and watching the ferocious competition between them to get it. Cinnamon being light and fast on her feet got it most of the time. But Honey had her own method; she would throw her full heavy weight on Cinnamon and in the struggle the ball could dislodge itself from her mouth, and then that was her chance to grab it. Plodding her way back to Miriam, she would ward off Cinnamon's attempt to seize the ball back from her by wiggling her stout body around like a first class contortionist. Miriam loved watching the dogs compete.

But today she was distracted by her thoughts, and Honey had to nudge her every now and then to get the game going again. She was thinking of Mr. Bruno's face when he came back from answering the phone. It was like a dark cloud, and his good hand was shaking. She pretended to be concentrating on studying the map because she thought he might feel embarrassed that she could see the ugly darkness around him; but then it occurred to her that he was probably not even aware of what she was noticing. So she glanced at him every now and again and saw that he was completely taken up by his own thoughts, with the darkness around him getting more and more dense. It wasn't a pretty sight and she was beginning to feel very uncomfortable, wanting to get away from him. She had not seen him like *that* before and it worried her.

When the geography lesson had finished he told her:

"My son Ben is coming to visit. I want you to make the bed up in the spare room."

Miriam saw some bronze and gold autumn leaves enfolding a dry cone on a Protea tree. That would make a nice arrangement for Ben's room she thought, and stepped into the long, dead grass to pick it. The dogs followed her like two guards, with saliva dripping tongues hanging from their open mouths. It was quite hard to get the cone off the tree and she had no scissors with her. She went round the bush to get a better grip of it. There was a sudden rustle in the grass and the dogs stopped dead, the hair on their backs rising.

Slowly it lifted its head out of the grass, its long body arching: a cobra.

All at once she was aware of a Presence surrounding her. The voice was very clear in her head: *Don't move! You are protected; no harm will come to you.*

The venomous tongue was flicking at the speed of lightning. Cinnamon whined slightly and her legs trembled as she moved around the snake to attack from the back. The Cobra's head followed the movement and sunk its fangs into Cinnamon's leg just before she crushed its head. The dying snake slithered frantically from side to side flattening the faded grass. Cinnamon stood panting; saliva streaming from her mouth, her legs buckling.

Miriam turned on her heels and ran, screaming all the time: "Anti serum! Anti serum! Bring it quickly. Cinnamon has been bitten!" Filamon heard her first and relayed the message, his voice booming across the smallholding. Katrina, who was taking the washing in heard, and ran into the house where Bruno was sitting talking to Ben who had arrived while Miriam was out walking.

"Master, the serum, Cinnamon, the snake - it's got her!!"

"In the top drawer of the dresser Ben, quick!"

Ben ran and met Filamon halfway up the drive. He handed the packet over and saw Filamon sprint across the field like a Zulu warrior. By the time Ben got to the dog and the dead snake, Cinnamon had had the serum and lay panting and shaking. Then he saw the girl standing wide eyed staring at the dog.

"Hello", he said. You must be, eh, what's your name again?"

"Miriam."

"Ah yes, Miriam." Unashamedly he scanned her from top to toe, then, "My God, you're going to be a beauty one day."

Miriam cast her eyes down and blushed scarlet. She knelt down by the dog and stroked its head.

"She saved my life," she said. "Do you think she'll live?"

Ben tore his eyes away from Miriam and knelt down too. He felt the dog's pulse and examined it.

"Only time will tell", he said, "but I think she might. How old are you Miriam?"

"Twelve," Miriam said and blushed again.

A squeaking reached their ears. It was Katrina pushing a wheelbarrow. They lifted Cinnamon onto it and slowly, almost reverently Filamon pushed her towards home. The other three followed; a respectful procession. Only Honey waddled in front of the wheelbarrow, as if leading the way. Bruno was waiting on the veranda.

"I've 'phoned the vet. He'll be here soon."

They laid the dog in her basket and covered her up with her blanket.

"You've acted very sensibly Miriam," Bruno said. "If Cinnamon pulls through, it will be thanks to your quick reaction."

"She saved my life, Mr. Bruno."

They heard a vehicle coming up the driveway. Ben went out to meet Dr. Brown and showed him in. Miriam stood anxiously next to the basket while he examined the dog.

"Will she live?" her voice was thin and shaky.

"I think she might, but I'd like to take her with me for tonight at least, in case of complications. Easier that way."

Filamon helped lift the dog into the van and Dr. Brown drove off. Miriam stood waving at it until Mr. Bruno said: "She'll be O.K. Miriam."

Suddenly she felt stupid, waving at a dog that can't even see her. When she turned to go inside, she caught

Ben's eyes on her. She hurried into the house so that Mr. Bruno would not see her blushing.

That night in bed Miriam was reliving her meeting with Ben, savouring his words: *My God, you're going to be a beauty one day!* She could see him in her mind's eye: tall and slim with hair the colour of the sand on the beach in Durban; and those very blue eyes that looked as if they were teasing all the time, but a nice playful teasing. No one had ever looked at her the way he had looked at her. She was aware of strange feelings, feelings that she had not known before. There was a golden glow around her heart and it felt like her whole body was tingling. It was so nice; it made her want to be with Ben. She didn't want to be in bed while Mr. Bruno and Ben were still up, talking in the lounge. She could hear their voices; Ben's voice had such a friendly tone to it. Oh, she needed to be near him, just near him. She got out of bed and crept to the door dividing the bedroom area from the lounge. Ben was saying: "… research psychology, very useful for industry."

Mr. Bruno was clearing his throat the way he did when he was dissatisfied with something she or Katrina had done in the house.

"Ben man, I don't know about this psychology thing. Really, it seems to me a pretty useless subject – all speculations and Mickey Mouse research, such an in-between thing. I mean, literature is literature and doesn't have to be proved, and scientific evidence can be verified. If I were to put up more money for your studies, it would have to be for a worthwhile study." There was a long silence. Then Ben's voice came, and Miriam heard that it wasn't friendly any more. She wondered what his eyes looked like when his voice was like that.

"What is it that you're afraid of that psychology will lay bare in you, Dad?"

Mr. Bruno snorted. "Afraid of!! I'm not afraid of some nut's theories about the human psyche, whatever that is."

"You're in denial Dad."

"Ha, ha, denial of what?"

"Of your suppressed anger."

"Ben, as usual, you're talking through your arsehole man!"

"See, you're so angry now Dad, if you could have got up out of that chair, you'd knock the shit out of me, as your dad did to you, and his dad did to him, and as you did to my mother."

"Oh, so that's how it is! She's put you up to this, hasn't she? She's poisoned your mind against me, as she's done all these years so that I hardly ever saw you as you grew up!"

"Mum had nothing to do with this Dad! It was just not very nice being with you. You always wanted to force me to do what *you* thought was right, just as you're doing now. You'll pay for my studies if I study what *you* think I ought to study, regardless of where my interests lay. Control, control, control! That's your whole life!"

Miriam couldn't imagine what Ben's eyes would look like when he shouted like *that*. Mr. Bruno's voice came high pitched and harsh and she hardly recognized it.

"That's how you've always been Ben - if you can't get your own way then you get shitty, throwing insults around. There's no point in talking to you, I'm going to bed."

Miriam shifted herself to her bedroom fast, wondering what to make of what she had overheard; trying to picture Ben's angry face, but it was impossible. She hoped he wouldn't look like Mr. Bruno when his frown was long and ugly. Perhaps Ben would still look as lovely as he looked in her head.

The next morning Mr. Bruno wasn't at the breakfast table, and there was no place laid for him either. Katrina said he was ill and had given orders to be left alone. Miriam and Ben had their breakfast together, and her heart had that golden feeling around it again. Ben didn't take much notice of her, just ate his porridge in silence, so she asked him if he'd heard any news about Cinnamon. He looked at her as if he'd been called away from another world, and then his face brightened.

"No Miriam, I haven't. Would you like me to phone up after breakfast?"

That made Miriam felt pretty good. People didn't usually ask her what she would like; they just gave orders, or told her what they were going to do.

"Yes please Ben," she said, and felt the heat coming up to her face again. It was saying his name that did it, it made her feel real grownup, and very close to him. He looked at her kindly and smiled, and she felt all those tingling feelings in her body again. She looked down at her porridge because it was all too much for her. She felt that she had to say something:

"If Mr. Bruno is ill, then perhaps there won't be lessons today."

"I guess not," Ben, wasn't looking at her, and for a moment it felt as if she was forgotten; but then his eyes came back to her "What would you do with that time?"

That was a new thought to her; she hadn't had time where she could choose what to do at Mr. Bruno's house. But she knew very quickly what she would do if Mr. Bruno wasn't telling her what to do.

"I'll paint."

"You'll paint? Do you like painting?"

She nodded.

"Have you done many paintings?"

"Uh huh"

"May I see some of them?"

Her heart expanded and she felt six feet tall. She had never felt like this in all her life. Not even when God stood on the mountain and listened to her telling him her secrets. That was when she decided to show Ben her eagle. She slipped of her chair and went to fetch it from her bedroom. She didn't excuse herself first, because she knew Ben wouldn't mind. When she came back, she spread it out on the table next to his plate. He put his spoon down, pushed his plate to one side, and picked the picture up. He looked at it for a long time without saying a word, and she was just beginning to think that perhaps he didn't like it, and that she should rather have shown him the picture of the mountain and the sky, or the one of the garden when he said:

"I think this picture comes from your heart."

Miriam hadn't thought of it like that, but she liked what she heard, and the words just tumbled out.

"It protects me."

Ben eyes narrowed as he leaned forward, looking at her closely.

"Protects you from what?"

She hesitated. "From the loneliness."

He let his breath out, and leaned back in his chair.

"From the loneliness. You find it very lonely here?"

A half forgotten sadness had come over her. She sniffed slightly. "Yes, I miss my schoolmates and Aunty Lizzie, Mr. de Wit too, and sometimes I wonder what Sandra and Bessie are doing."

She saw Ben pursing his lips tightly together and frown; then he looked at the picture again.

"You've got talent, Miriam." And after a while, "You should always paint from your heart."

They didn't speak any more, just sat in silence, a comfortable silence, and when that golden feeling expanded her heart, she said:

"I would like to make a picture of you Ben."

That was the second time she had said his name, and this time she didn't blush. At first Ben said nothing, but his eyes enlarged and a light came into them, and she knew that that was exactly how she would want to paint him. At last he said:

"I was going to leave this morning Miriam. How long would it take you?"

She couldn't bear the thought of Ben leaving and without thinking she said.

"It will be terribly lonely if you leave," her voice became tearful, "and Cinnamon is not even home!"

"Oh yes, Cinnamon. Let me go and find out how she's doing."

He got up from the table and just then Katrina came in from the bedrooms to say that Mr. Bruno wanted to see Ben. Miriam wanted to stand outside the door to listen, but Katrina was making the beds, and she would see her, so she went to her room and just sat there.

After a while she heard the rumbling of a car coming up the dirt track and saw that it was Dr. Brown's van. She rushed towards it as soon as it had stopped. Dr. Brown opened the back door and Cinnamon jumped out and up at her.

"Cinnie, Cinnie!" she shouted, and stroked her until Honey pushed in to be stroked too. Ben came out and shook hands with Dr. Brown.

"She's made it then."

"Yeah, she'll be OK now, but it was a close shave."

"Coffee?" Ben asked

"No thanks, the practice awaits. Are you stopping long?"

"Just a couple of days until my dad is better, he's had a bit of a set back," Ben said, looking uncomfortable.

Miriam's heart was singing, Ben was not going to leave today. Hurrah!!! When they went into the house Katrina had cleared the breakfast table and had set it up for school. Ben turned to her.

"My dad wants me to be your teacher for now. I believe we start with the maths."

"Yes, the painting lesson doesn't come until after I've worked on my essay on Tuesdays."

"So I believe", Ben said and she noticed him pursing his lips together again.

And so it happened that over the next two days Miriam was able to paint Ben, because Ben wasn't bothering with the school lessons, he just sat and let her paint him. She painted him with the light in his eyes, even though the light was no longer there, but she liked the sadness around his mouth too, so she painted that also.

When at last she showed Ben the picture, he looked at it for a long, long time, then:

"Is that how I look to you? *That* sad?"

She nodded and waited for him to see what he saw in the eagle picture.

"I like it, he said at last. There is *something* in it." He looked puzzled.

"You told me to always paint from the heart."

That was when the light came back, into his eyes.

"Like that", she said, "just like you look now."

"How do I look now?"

"With light in your eyes."

He put the picture on the sideboard and stepped back looking at it intensely. After a long while he said:

"You're a remarkable young lady Miriam."

Miriam felt as if she could float up into the air, and sail over the mountaintop, just like her eagle.

On the morning after the quarrel with Ben, when Bruno tried to move from his bed into his wheelchair to go to the bathroom, he realized that his legs were much weaker than they had been the night before when he left Ben in anger. So after his ablutions he went straight back to bed. When Katrina brought his coffee in he gave orders not to be disturbed. His emotions were in turmoil and he felt deeply unhappy. Thoughts were swirling around in his head and phrases kept coming back to him: *hit the shit out of me, like your dad did to you, and his dad to him!* But the bit, *like you did to my mother,* was the one that plunged him into darkness. He swung his working arm around a few times, just to assure himself that he still had control over it. What if he lost complete control over his legs? What if he couldn't get himself into his wheelchair any more? He felt like he was going to be sucked into a cesspit and he was too weak to prevent it. *If Ben hadn't come this wouldn't have happened*, he thought bitterly. Or even if he had just let Ben have the bloody money for his so called scientific degree and not made his views known. But he had, and the quarrel had happened.

He moved his legs around. They were still working, nothing like the lame hand, but they were decidedly weaker. Perhaps if he rested them for a couple of days the strength would come back into them. *But what about Miriam's lessons?* He didn't like her to idle around the place. That would do her no good: S*he's beginning to get to the age where one has to keep a firm grip.* He heard Katrina working in the bedroom section and called out to her.

"Katrina, tell Ben to come and see me."

When Ben came in and he saw the guilty look in his eyes, he took courage.

"Ben, I'm concerned about Miriam. I don't want her lessons to be interrupted and I'm going to need a few days to recover." He noticed how Ben's discomfort deepened at the word 'recover'. "I wonder if you'll be so good as to stand in for me."

Ben hesitated, fumbling with his shirt buttons.

"I'm not a teacher Dad." His blue eyes swept across the carpet for a moment, then he looked up and sighed, "OK, I'll have a go."

Bruno felt slightly more in control.

"You'll find the timetable in the top drawer of the sideboard, the lessons marked out in the correct order. You can look at that later, but for today it is maths first, then literature, she's researching for an essay on whales, and then it is her art lesson. She's very proficient in that, all you need to do is set the materials out for her and make sure she stops when her time is up. She needs to stick to our routine."

When Ben left the room Bruno felt better. Things were under control in his household.

Bruno woke up on the Thursday morning, knowing that his legs had got some strength back in them. He had made up his mind that he would let Ben have the money. They could forget about the quarrel. Soon his life would be back to normal.

Ben and Miriam were sitting at the schoolroom table when he wheeled himself in at 10'oclock. They should be doing history now. He found them poring over Miriam's paintings, including the one of the eagle which she had hidden from him.

"Why are you not busy with your history lesson Miriam?" His voice was stern, but it had a tightness in it that gave away the wobble that he was suddenly thrown into.

"Because she has been busy painting a portrait of me." Ben's voice was defiant.

Bruno swung his wheelchair in underneath the table. "A portrait of you! In the time I had set for her education!"

"Take a look at this Dad, no history or geography or what ever could compare with this."

Bruno took the picture and saw from the corner of his eye Miriam furtively hiding the eagle. So she showed it to Ben but hid it from him. What have these two been up to while he wasn't there to keep things in check? He put the portrait against the flower vase so that he could view it from a distance. There was his son, looking at him with a light in his eyes that he had never seen before. Nor had he ever seen the sadness in Ben. The shivers ran down his spine. This was Ben all right, but a Ben he had not been aware off. He couldn't take his eyes off the picture, and he felt that the light in the eyes was penetrating into his very being, and it scared him. In a panic he put his hand onto his heart to stop it, and he felt as if the light was receding, hovering just outside his chest. All at once he remembered the dream, and intuitively he knew that if the light went out, he would be plunged into the most unbearable darkness. He took his hand away from his heart and turned to Miriam.

"I am touched by your painting Miriam."

Then he looked at it again. The light was coming at him. He looked away, turning to Ben.

"What do you think" he hesitated slightly, "how do you feel about it?"

"Feel seems the right word Dad. It seems to me all about feelings."

"Mm, perhaps, but there's more than feelings to it."

"Yes, what Dad? What else do you see there?" Ben's voice was full of intense anticipation.

Bruno swallowed at the lump in his throat that threatened to choke him, but he managed to squeeze the word out.

"Light."

"Light!" Ben and Miriam's voices were a duet.

Bruno nodded sheepishly.

Miriam clapped her hands.

"Mr. Bruno! You saw it straight away. It's fantastic! Ben didn't know what it was he saw, first of all he just saw the sadness."

The lump in Bruno's throat had vanished and now he felt part of the little group around the table.

"Yes, the sadness is there, but the light makes it all...well, bearable."

Bruno and Ben's eyes met across the table, and Bruno thought that he saw a glimmer of pride in the way that Ben looked at him, smiled at him. Could it be that Ben was, after all, proud of him? How was it that he never, until now, recognized the brightness in Ben's blue eyes? Eyes that can survive sadness. A slow smile spread across Bruno's face, meeting Ben's.

That night after Miriam was told that it was her bedtime, Bruno decided that going to bed a bit later than his usual time wouldn't hurt for once. He offered Ben a sherry and they sat watching TV. When the programme had finished Ben said:

"I will need to head off tomorrow. I'm back at work on Monday, and it's a long journey."

Bruno nodded. "I'll transfer the funds into your account every term."

"Thanks Dad, thanks very much." He got up and shook hands with Bruno, then on impulse bent down and hugged him.

In her bed Miriam was dreaming that the eagle was giving her a ride through the sky. She felt as if she were a cloud, going willingly wherever an invisible hand steered her.

Later that night, Bruno was twitching in his sleep. He was struggling through a vast marshy plain, an almost endless distance towards a beckoning light.

When Bruno told Miriam that she could ride into town on her new bicycle, she was over the moon. Her first thought when he gave her the key to his post box was that there might be a letter for her from Ben, and no one would know about it. When Aunty Lizzie's letters came, Mr. Bruno always knew about it, because he handed it to her. When she replied she had to give her letter to Mr. Flint, the nearest neighbour, to take to the post office.

She had lots of errands to do for Mr. Bruno, so she decided to do those first and go to the post office last, so that she wouldn't forget any of them in her excitement when she hid Ben's letter in her coat pocket. But when she came into town, she just couldn't wait to get his letter, and went to the post office first. There were a good few letters in the box, all brown window ones. She fancied Ben's letter would be in a bright coloured envelope. She felt deep into the box, just in case it had got stuck right at the back of it, but there was nothing. No letter from Ben.

She swallowed a few times, trying to get rid of the disappointment, kicking at the loose stones in the road as she walked on, head bent.

Mr. Bruno had explained to her where in the main street the General Dealer's store was, because he wanted her to buy him some vests. When she walked in there were a few people standing near the door: three men and a woman. She looked around the shop but could only see crockery, cutlery, and pots and pans. So she asked them where the clothing department was. The woman said: "Upstairs Honey." The men were silent, but she felt them looking at her in a funny way, which made her feel very uncomfortable, and yet somehow kind of excited. When she turned away towards the wide staircase, there was a snigger and some talk which she didn't quite hear, but then she heard one of the men said loudly, "Well lame legs doesn't mean everything is lame." Their laughter swooped towards her, making her feel dirty. She felt angry and humiliated, though she didn't quite know why.

When she came out of the shop they were gone, but when she loaded her shopping into the front basket, she noticed that one of them, a man with thick legs and a beer belly, was hanging around by his car, looking at her. So she decided to go away from the main street to the back street where she was told the Indian shops were, and where she was to buy spices for Mr. Bruno and some curtain material for her room. That was much better. She liked the colours in the Indian shops. Yards and yards of material, any colour one could think of, and the Indians talked nicely to her.

On her way back she stopped at the farm stall for vegetables and fruit. That also belonged to an Indian, serving behind the counter. His wife was putting jars of jam and other preserves on a side shelf. She looked at Miriam kindly and said:

"Whom are you buying all this stuff for?"

"For Mr. B, er, Mr. Mynhard."

"Ah, yes, Mr. Mynhard. I have heard that he now has extra help. How is he these days?"

It felt nice for Miriam talking to the Indian lady, and she liked the orange and gold of her sari.

"He has been ill in bed for a few days when his son Ben visited, but now he's better again," she said.

"His son visited?" She looked surprised.

Miriam nodded.

The Indian lady came out with her and helped her load the vegetables in the back basket.

"My, you *have* been shopping!" she said when she peeped into the front basket.

"Yes, Mr. Bruno said I could have new curtains made for my bedroom."

She smiled. "Is that what you call him? Mr. Bruno?"

"Yes: when I called him Mr. Mynhard, he told me that his name was Bruno, but I didn't feel I could call someone who was old enough to be Aunty Lizzie's dad by his first name."

"You sound like a really respectful young lady," she said, and her eyes looked gentle. "Who is Aunty Lizzie?"

The sadness came over Miriam again. "She's the one who brought me up in Mr. and Mrs. de Wit's house", and then the tears just welled up in her eyes without her being able to stop it. "Oh, I do miss her so much!"

The Indian lady put her arm around Miriam's shoulder. "Poor child," she said, "you must be so lonely."

Miriam nodded and wiped her nose with the back of her hand.

"I tell you what, I'll phone Mr. Mynhard up, and ask him if you could sometimes came and visit us. Would you like that?"

"Oh yes! But I don't think he will let me go. You see in the week we have school lessons, and over the weekends when Katrina is off, I have to cook and look after Mr. Bruno."

She touched Miriam's arm gently. "Don't you worry my dear, I'll talk with him; he knows us. In the school holidays you don't have lessons. What's your name?"

"Miriam. And yours?"

She gave Miriam a lovely smile. "Sunda"

When she rode off, she felt better even though she was still so sad that Ben hadn't written to her. *I gave him the picture I made of him,* she thought, *so now I don't even have that to look at.* But there was a little flame of hope in her that maybe next week he would write.

When she got home Mr. Bruno was just sitting down to his lunch.

"You're late Miriam," he said and frowned, that long frown that went right up his bald patch. "What kept you so long?"

"It takes time to choose material," she said. "There were so many different colours."

His face softened a bit. "Still, you're very late."

She felt she had to account for every minute.

"Sunda talked to me for a while also."

"Oh," he said. Then after he'd chewed the food in his mouth thoroughly, and had swallowed it, he said, "Sunda and Abdullah are very interesting people, they are Hindus."

"What are Hindus, Mr. Bruno?"

"That is a religion, like Christianity is a religion."

"Oh, do they also pray to God and read in the Bible like Mr. de Wit?"

"They have many Gods, Miriam, and their Bible is called the Vedas."

Miriam was intrigued, and started to fire questions, but he held up his hand.

"Not while we're eating Miriam, too much talk at dinner time isn't good for the digestion. What I'll do is prepare lessons for you on Hinduism for our cultural studies slot."

Miriam felt really cross with Mr. Bruno. *Why can't we just talk about it now?* She thought, *it sounded so interesting. Why must we always make a lesson out of everything?*

Bruno saw the expression on her face.

"No use sulking, you'll get all your answers in due course. But in the mean time, here's something to cheer you up. Ben has phoned, and he said to tell you that all his friends liked your picture of him, and his girlfriend thinks you're an exceptional artist."

For the first time Miriam was glad for the afternoon rest rule and went to her room straight away. She felt like she did once when Mr. and Mrs. de Wit took them to Durban and she rode high on a huge wave, shouting with the joy of it, and in the next moment was crushed down and whirled about as if she was in a washing machine.

She stuck her head under her pillow, and cried, and cried, and cried. Then she listened for the sound of the eagle, but there was nothing, nor did the voice came into her head to console her. *Perhaps it's a good thing that I haven't got Ben's picture any more* she thought, *it would have just reminded me of how much I miss him.*

Bruno was sitting by the table on the veranda preparing the lesson on cultural studies for Miriam, but his heart was not in it. He had never been able to swallow this thing called religion. Of course he had to pretend that he was a devout Christian when he was a schoolmaster, and when he was headmaster, he had to lead the Monday morning assembly, read from the Bible, and pray to a God that he had no contact with at all. That was if such a Being existed. That was what he liked about science. *Theories can be proved, can give one something tangible to get hold of.* Yet, neither science nor God had been able to cure him, or even stop his decline.

He thought of Ben and his psychology, and his assertion that his father was full of suppressed anger. In fact, he had been thinking about that a lot ever since Ben left. With Ben out of the way, he felt safe enough to look at the accusation. True, he did feel anger and resentment towards his father. But then, was that not a justified anger? Yet, even if his anger was justified, how did it help him? How did it free him?

He stared out across the valley and saw the birds swirling around in circles. They were like his thoughts; going round and round endlessly. At least the birds could break free and shoot off into another direction, but he felt trapped in his mind; in endless thought. An idea popped into his head: perhaps his father had felt that his anger towards *his* father was justified too, and that's why he refused to go to him while he lay dying. Again, it didn't help him either, just drove him further into the bottle. Then it struck him: Ben was right, there was a pattern here - anger and discord between father and son, passed down from generation to generation. He stared at the mountain in amazement without seeing it, thinking: that is what it said in the Bible he was forced to read. Something like God saying he would visit the sins of the fathers onto the son, into the third and fourth generation. So he was carrying his father's sins, *and* his grandfather's and God knows how *he* came to be so angry. What a God! Punishing, punishing, punishing!

Bruno saw Miriam coming up the path with the dogs in tow. *She* didn't even know who her ancestors were, he thought. She didn't know from whom she got her intelligence and talents. For the first time he wondered how Miriam felt inside herself. How did she cope with what life had dealt her?

The dogs ran ahead of Miriam and nuzzled up to him. He stroked their heads absentmindedly. Miriam came onto the veranda and took her straw hat off. On impulse he said:

"Miriam, do you believe in God?"

Miriam stopped dead in her tracks, her eyes wide, scanning his face. It took some time before she answered.

"Which one?"

"Which one? How do you mean?"

Miriam scrutinized his face further before deciding on an approach.

"Well, Mr. Bruno, you said yourself that the Hindu religion has many Gods." She pulled a chair up and sat next to him.

He smiled. "Oh I see, but you were brought up with the Christian faith. Do you believe in the God the Bible tells us about?"

Miriam sounded defiant. "Do you have to believe in the God of the faith you were taught as a child?"

Bruno stroked Honey's head, and his voice was very gentle when he answered: "No Miriam, you don't have to."

He could see her relax a bit, but for a while she still watched his face like one would a sparring partner, and then she let out a deep breath and said:

"When I was younger, I believed God was that rock on the mountain on Mr. and Mrs. de Wit's side that looked like a man. I often talked to him, and I believed he would keep me safe." She paused. "But he didn't."

"He didn't?"

Miriam shook her head. "He let me be taken away from him, and from Aunty Lizzie, and from my school mates."

She sat hunched up, and Bruno felt a shockwave going through his body. So this was how she felt about being here. He had never realized! He thought this would be to her benefit. He could educate her well, and gave her material well being. He had no words. He felt totally impotent to handle the situation, until a thought struck him.

"Yet God kept you safe when the snake could have killed you."

Miriam straightened herself; defiant again.

"Oh, it wasn't *that* God, it was the inside voice that always helps me when I'm desperate."

The word 'desperate' hit Bruno like a rock, but he recovered himself quickly, and got his thoughts back on track.

"You have another God, who lives inside you?"

Miriam looked at him in amazement, then towards the mountain with a thoughtful expression on her face.

"Oh perhaps *that* is God then. Aunty Lizzie *said* he would live in my heart when I come here."

Bruno felt he was treading on hallowed ground.

"Aunty Lizzie sounds like a wise woman, and the God in your heart sounds very caring and friendly."

Miriam looked at him and smiled, totally trusting now. She leaned towards him as if they were two conspirators.

"Sometimes the voice and the white eagle come together. But with the snake it was only the voice."

Bruno swallowed.

"I'm so very glad you're alive Miriam."

There was real emotion in his voice. At that moment he did not feel they were teacher and pupil, just two humans groping their way through life.

"Where does your God live Mr. Bruno?"

In front of the enquiring green eyes, Bruno felt himself a pauper, deeply ashamed of his spiritual rags.

"Miriam, I don't know, I can't find Him," he said almost pleadingly, and he felt like adding, P*erhaps it's just as well, because if I did, He's sure to be very angry*, but he held that back.

Spontaneously Miriam picked up his lame hand and stroked it.

"Poor Mr. Bruno," she said.

CHAPTER 5

Bruno felt himself in a dilemma greater than anything he had ever faced. He realized that he had become very attached to Miriam. In his affections she could almost have been Amelie. He wouldn't have wanted Amelie to feel 'desperate' or to doubt God because 'He let her be taken away from him'. He needed Miriam because of his physical condition, but now he realized that he needed her for far more than that. There was an irrepressible joy in her, which alleviated her sadness and pain. He thought of the picture she had painted of Ben, the light in it, and he felt certain that Ben's light could only have been seen and brought to life because of the light in her. She had the power to home in on the good in people. She had made him see his son as he had not seen him before, which brought about the beginnings of a better relationship between them. She gave structure and meaning to his days, and he was holding her here against her own wishes, like a caged bird. The thought was unbearable, but so was the thought of letting her go.

There was another feeling that hovered on the edge of his awareness, and it made him cringe with shame, so that he suppressed it immediately. When Miriam's compassionate little hand stroked his lame hand, it stirred up long forgotten feelings in him. The physical touch, and the spiritual intimacy between them that had happened so spontaneously, shattered his rigid boundaries. Longings and passions were seeping through, making him feel frightened and uncomfortable, so that he forced himself to focus on the practical side of his dilemma.

If he could bring Lizzie here, replace Katrina with her, then Miriam would have one of her longings fulfilled. Perhaps the schoolmates would not be so important then. Immediately he saw his sister's face in front of him. She would be furious. Lizzie ran her household for her just the way she wanted it. Then there was Katrina to consider as well. She would lose her job, and would not be very likely to find another one so well paid. She spoke only a smattering of English and her dour disposition did not make her very employable in this area. He employed her because he knew she wasn't likely to leave him, and she would obey his commands exactly. Her family home was near by, so he hadn't had to supply accommodation for her. What about Lizzie? Would she want to come and work for him? At Daniel and Kate's she had her own little place, while here she would always be in his house, even on her days off.

As the vague discomfort in him grew to a point of almost panic, he knew he had to get Lizzie to come and live in this house, or else he had to send Miriam back to Kate and Daniel. That thought plunged him into the depth of despair.

After a sleepless night, Bruno decided on what he saw as the lesser of the evils. His good hand shook as he picked up the telephone receiver, while his lame hand lay dreamily on his lap. Daniel answered. He was glad; Daniel might just understand. They talked about this and that, until Daniel asked if he thought Miriam had settled down well. This was an opening for Bruno.

"Well, actually," and then the fear that they might take Miriam back, made him change tack. "Actually, she's settled remarkably well and is making great strides in her education. She is an intelligent girl who can really benefit greatly from the individual tuition she is receiving."

"I'm glad," Daniel said.

"But there is one hitch Dan." He paused to lend weight to his request. "She misses Lizzie something terrible. I guess Lizzie had become a mother figure to her, and a girl of her age needs a mother to guide her through puberty."

Daniel sighed. "Exactly what I said to Kate, when she insisted we send her over to help you, and Lizzie hasn't been herself either lately. She looks pale and drawn, and has become very withdrawn."

Bruno took heart. "Wouldn't it be best if Lizzie came to work here?"

"Ooh! You know Kate: all hell will be let loose if you took Lizzie from here."

"Maybe it would not be me who took her away. What if Lizzie herself wants to come and work for me to be near Miriam."

"Ah, now - we've got to be very careful here. If Lizzie really insists on being with Miriam, Kate might bring her back here."

Bruno's heart sank to an all time low. "Well, I guess it's not all that serious", he said quickly. "No doubt Miriam will adapt to the situation. Perhaps we just need to give it a bit more time."

That night at supper, facing Miriam across the table, Bruno thought of something.

"Did your Aunty Lizzie say when her next yearly holiday would be?"

"It's always in the long school holidays when Mr. and Mrs. de Wit and Sandra and Bessie go away. Sometimes they took me with them."

"What did your Aunty Lizzie do, did she go and visit her family?"

"No, she always just stayed in our little house. I don't know if she's got family."

"I see. Do you think this year she might like to come and visit us? She could stay in the spare room, and we could get another bicycle so that the two of you could ride into town, and have fun together."

Miriam's face lit up, and her innocence made Bruno see his own conniving as if through a magnifying glass.

"Yeah!! I'm sure she'd like that!"

"Well then, why don't you write to her tonight? Tell her no one needs to know, it can be just between us."

It took Bruno a few days to adjust to having a guest in the house, and to not have his mornings structured by his well-organized school lessons. He also had to cope with loneliness, and feeling at a loss when Miriam and Lizzie rode off to town on their bicycles, but he was determined to win Lizzie's approval, and to make her feel welcome. Even if she didn't want to come and work for him, he needed her to give a good report of how good Miriam had it with him.

However, he was aware of a certain reticence in Lizzie, which caused a strain on the time the three of them were together. Sometimes he wished she hadn't come, and that he and Miriam could be alone together again. He could then sit with her when she painted, or just talk with her, but Lizzie was here, and he had to keep reminding himself that his goal was to persuade her to come and work for him; and also that Miriam would not be looking so happy and full of life if she wasn't here.

It was in the second week of Lizzie's visit that Miriam got a sore throat and a temperature. Lizzie insisted that she stayed in bed and got as much sleep as possible. She herself liked to sit on the veranda, working on the cardigan she was knitting for Miriam. Bruno came out onto the veranda too, and immediately there was tension in the air again. Nevertheless Bruno decided to put some feelers out.

"You've been with my sister and brother-in-law for a long time, haven't you Lizzie? I don't think anyone else has ever stayed that long."

"I stayed there because Miriam was there. I wanted to bring her up."

The resentment in her voice caused it to quiver, and Bruno could feel his heart thumping. This was dangerous territory.

"You've done a very good job of it Lizzie."

"My job wasn't finished. Miriam was only twelve."

Bruno saw his chance.

"Yes, and she needs a mother. I realize that now. Before, I didn't think of it."

Lizzie pursed her lips together and focused on her knitting.

"I'd very much like you to continue bringing her up, here in my house Lizzie. How would you feel about that?"

Lizzie's knitting dropped on her lap, as she stared at Bruno.

"You want me to take Katrina's job?"

Bruno blushed.

"I'll find work for her. You could have the spare room, and Miriam would have a mother again."

Lizzie's face stayed clouded. She was silent for a while, and when she spoke her voice was really shaky.

"Why Mr. Mynhard, why did you have to take Miriam? You could have hired someone to come and sleep in at nights. Why take a child?"

Yes why indeed a child? Bruno was stroking his chin. True Kate suggested it or else he would never have thought of it. And of course the idea of teaching again, appealed to him. Yet, inside himself he felt that that wasn't the whole story.

He spoke very softly when he replied.

"My little girl died when she was not so very much younger than Miriam, and my boy was taken away from me. I guess I have a need for a child."

Lizzie opened her eyes wide as she stared at Bruno.

"Oh. Oh." Then, with a voice that had lost its quiver: "I understand Mr. Mynhard."

The resentment had fallen from her, the air on the veranda seemed fresh and clear. Cinnamon, who lay stretched out on the floor sleeping, suddenly thumped her tail as if she was welcoming an old friend.

"Do you Lizzie?"

"For sure Mr. Mynhard."

Bruno scrutinized her face.

"And you Lizzie, how come you're so devoted to Miriam?"

Lizzie cast her eyes down. "Same reason Mr. Mynhard."

"Same reason?"

"I don't ever talk about the death of my baby, because when Miriam came, my baby came alive in my heart."

Bruno took a deep breath. He could feel his hand shaking.

"I see. I didn't know that." And after a few moments; "Looks like we're both in the same boat."

When Lizzie's eyes met Bruno's, it seemed to him that her soul was shining though them.

"Yes Mr. Mynhard, we both need Miriam."

There was a storm, of course there was a storm, and Kate accused Bruno of underhandedness, of betraying his own sister. She threatened to take Miriam back and ban Lizzie from ever seeing her again. But Daniel stepped in.

"Listen Kate, you're the one who suggested we send Miriam to Bruno. You didn't care about Lizzie or Miriam's feelings – dismissed it when I brought that up."

"Well, I did say it needed only be temporarily until Bruno could make better arrangements."

Daniel smirked slightly. "Well, I've got news for you: In actual fact, Bruno can make no better arrangements than this."

Kate looked at him as if he'd gone out of his mind. "But he's got plenty of money…

"It has nothing to do with money! Bruno and I had a heart to heart talk." Daniel took a deep breath and when he spoke again his voice was very gentle. "You've never lost a child. Bruno has lost two. For him having Miriam is like having Amelie back again."

Kate was silent for a moment, "But why take Lizzie away from me? From his own sister!" She pouted sullenly.

"Kate, he isn't taking Lizzie away. Do you not see how she is pining? She was going to leave us in any case to try and find work nearer where she could see Miriam more often." He paused for a moment; "To Lizzie, Miriam is like her own child. You're a mother yourself, can you not understand that?"

Kate's eyes softened slightly.

"Yes", she said at last. "I guess this way they can share the child they both wanted."

"Exactly."

"But I will miss Lizzie", she said in a weepy voice, sniffing and wiping her nose, "she is my right hand. Bruno needn't think I'll be going to visit *him* in a hurry again."

Daniel shook his head and sighed. Kate was not one to let go of what she wanted easily. For him there were mixed feelings: sadness and gratitude. He was sad that it was the end of an era in his household. He was genuinely fond of Miriam, and what he had hoped to be a temporary arrangement, he now knew was permanent. He was grateful though that Miriam seemed to have better opportunities with Bruno, and also would be with her beloved Aunty Lizzie to guide her through puberty. He would be able to follow her progress, the progress of that little baby he picked up from the doorstep.

When Lizzie packed up her belongings, feelings were swirling around in her. This had been her home since she was twenty, nearly thirteen years ago, and she had shared it with Miriam for twelve years. True, it was not her own, and could never compare to the home Joshua had provided for her, but in this home she was safe. She and Miriam had to themselves more space than her whole family ever had. It was kept in good condition at no cost to her. Yes, she had to work hard for the privilege, and Miriam too had to lend a hand, but all in all, she was much better off than in Joshua's house.

But when Miriam left, everything changed. The enormous effort she had made to help Miriam hold on to her faith had kept her afloat for a while, but then faded and darkness descended: she was back under the shadow of Table Mountain, sitting staring at a puzzling world, yet not seeing it, nor comprehending. Now, as then, she wondered why she was going on – there was nothing to live for.

She went down with bronchitis and lay in her bed exhausted, hardly able to cope with the cough that ripped through her body. Somehow it reminded her of her labour pains, and she desperately tried to blank the memory out. She fell to uttering hoarse sounds: 'Hallelujah, merciful God, hallelujah.' She was a little girl again, clapping her hands, imitating her mother's supplications for a better life.

Daniel de Wit sent for the doctor and Sandra was appointed to look after her needs for food such as it was, and to check that she had taken her medicine. On the fifth day when the fever had left her and she lay staring at the mountain, she saw the upright rock – Miriam's God - and suddenly she knew why she had to go on living. She dared not die. How could she do that to a child? She felt ashamed of herself and got up on wobbly legs to wash and dress. When the cough had subsided she wrote to Miriam and promised that she would write to her every week. Then she sat down and looked at her savings, her monthly income and her outgoings, and decided that she could manage to pay for a taxi once a month to go and see her.

When she came back from her first visit, and went about her duties in Kate de Wit's household she could barely look at her. Deep down there was a terrible resentment towards this woman and her disabled brother. More and more now at night she would dream of Joshua, and his face would suddenly turn into Mrs. de Wit's face before it would be superimposed by Mr. Mynhard's. Yet she had to hide this resentment, especially towards Mr. Mynhard, as she was well aware of his reluctance to let her visit Miriam in her prison of his routine.

And now everything had changed and she was going to run Mr. Mynhard's household and be with Miriam again. But there was a price: she would lose her home, her and Miriam's privacy, and she would be subjected to Mr. Mynhard's rules and routine. It seemed to her that she would never escape the fate of her family - always living in other people's houses. Even what she thought of as her home as Joshua's wife, had in reality been his home where he could make and break as he pleased, and where he chose to break.

As she packed the last of her belongings, she felt angry: angry that the long suppressed thoughts and feelings about Joshua had been stirred up. Seeing Miriam's God through the window, the God that she had saluted on the day she left, it came to her that the rock God Miriam had left behind to look after her, was perhaps not much different from the benevolent Presence that she believed had given Miriam to her in the first place – a God who came in the shape of one's needs of the moment. She took a last long look at the mountain, and God. Then she carried her suitcase and boxes to the pickup point of the taxi.

Bruno was pleasantly surprised at how smoothly Lizzie had slotted into his household. There was very little upheaval and the months just rolled by, one after the other. However, Lizzie wasn't Katrina. On some subtle level he and Lizzie were sparring partners. Lizzie's strength was Miriam's love for her, and her ability to run his household well. His strength obviously, was his material wealth and his ability to pay Lizzie well, and to support and educate Miriam. He was also vaguely aware of a trump card that he was able to play when he needed to. Paradoxically his 'strength', lay in his weakness. He had seen the compassion in Miriam's eyes whenever she looked at his lame hand. It was almost as if that hand was steering her whenever she got obstreperous. As if it had a life of its own, it would somehow become prominent when Miriam was trying to break free of the household routine that meant so much to him. Lizzie too had an understanding of how his plight made him cling to the regularity of his days, and often she would gently guide Miriam back on track.

The lame hand was the ruling hand.

Yet Lizzie, in her own way, had managed to make changes to their days. She had become friendly with Sunda and Abdullah, and during the school holiday breaks they came to visit. Sunda's friendliness filled his home and he couldn't object. Besides it was good to sit quietly on the veranda talking to Abdullah who knew a lot about growing crops.

"Where did you learn all this Abdullah?" he had once asked.

"Long time ago I worked for the growers in Johannesburg."

"Oh, dangerous place that," he shuddered.

"Yes," Abdullah pointed to the hand, "you'd never leave a valuable thing like that out in the open. How did you come by it?"

"Years ago a fellow, an artist, came up to the house selling some of his stuff. I bought that and a couple of paintings from him."

Lizzie, who had been chatting to Sunda in the kitchen, brought tea and a freshly baked cake out. He so appreciated her cooking, the carrot cake she had made was just as he liked it: moist, sweetened with fat juicy raisins.

Yes, Lizzie had her subtle strengths too, that was clear. She even persuaded him to accept Sunda and Abdullah's invitation to be taken out for a drive through the lovely countryside. They stopped at the curio shop where he bought Lizzie a double string of beads and Miriam chose a hand carved brooch from the animal collection. Afterwards they had tea at Sunda and Abdullah's house; he marvelled at the smells of exotic spices.

There was a change in Miriam too, which was gratifying. It seemed the new set up with Lizzie in charge of the housekeeping gave her more confidence - a broadening out of herself. Lizzie had more time to do things with Miriam during school holidays than she had in the de Wit's household – three people were easier to care for than six. Sometimes he was drawn into their activities and sometimes he just sat and watched. Even the school terms seemed busier and more interesting than before, and it was quite a few months before she asked for the promised lesson on Hindu religion. He dutifully prepared it and that morning they had it. To his surprise he enjoyed it very much. Her enthusiasm and interest in the subject brushed aside the dry facts and she started firing questions at him about reincarnation. Their lesson became a discussion and exploration of how it sat with her, and of how he viewed it. He felt stimulated, and when he came in from his daily inspection of Filamon's work, he was in high spirits. He was still chewing it over in his mind when he found a hole in the wire mesh of the chicken run. Filamon had neglected to mend it, and he saw the big red hen poking her head through. Somehow that was not such a big deal today. He saw Filamon standing on the other side of the pen, watering some shrubs.

"Filamon!" he called, his voice calm and pleasant, "There's a hole here in the wire mesh, it needs mending."

Filamon stopped his chanting. "Yebo Master", then resumed his song.

Bruno was just mounting the veranda when he heard the telephone ring. The living room area was empty, and he assumed Miriam and Lizzie had gone to their rooms.

Daniel's voice on the other end of the line sounded worried:

"I was hoping to catch you before you go for your rest Bruno."

"I'm just about to."

"Listen man, eh…" Daniel sounded unusually hesitant, "I'm not quite sure what to do. There's a woman here who claims she's Miriam's mother."

Bruno felt himself go cold. "Miriam's mother! Oh my God. Can this be true? What's she like?"

"Very smartly dressed, beads in the braided hair…"

"No, I mean, how does she come across as a person?"

"Quite aggressive, asked me if I was the boss of the orphanage, and when I said yes, she said: *What happened to my baby I left here on the doorstep!* God, there's so many thoughts in my mind now. I asked her to take a seat on the veranda and said that I would go and find out for her. Where are we going from here Bruno?"

"Is she still there?" Bruno asked to win time.

"Yes, of course, I can see her now through the window, sitting stiffly, clutching her snakeskin handbag."

"What are our legal rights Daniel?"

"Legal rights? Well yes, of course Kate and I are Miriam's foster parents, and officially she is just visiting you for the purposes of education. She's under the age of sixteen, so she can't just be taken away from us, but that's not the point Bruno. Do we have the right to withhold this from Miriam? I mean, morally? Does she not have the right to know who her parents are?"

Apart from his shaking hand holding the telephone, Bruno sat very still. Even his mind had become quiet, like a mountaineer whose life depended on focussing fully on the present moment. There were no room for speculations, thoughts about past or future. Eventually he said,

"Daniel, tell her that her baby is with foster parents, and that you will try and find out about her whereabouts." Bruno's voice was very firm; he was the schoolmaster giving an order. "It will give us time to work out the moral issues that you've raised. There's a lot at stake here Daniel. We need time."

Daniel was quiet on the other end of the line, and Bruno continued,

"You know now how Lizzie feels about Miriam, you know what she means to me, but most importantly, how will all this affect Miriam? She's going to be thirteen in two months time. Is this a time for her to deal with an issue as big as this? We need time Daniel!" he repeated.

"But the woman could find out from somewhere else you know. The facts are glaring: a coloured baby found on a doorstep, it doesn't happen every five minutes in this area. Everyone around here knows that we have fostered her, and that she's now with you."

"It will still give us some time."

Daniel saw that the woman had got up from her chair and was pacing the veranda. He also heard a car in the distance. It might be Kate coming home.

"OK Bruno, I'll tell her."

Bruno put the phone down and went straight to his room, but he didn't get onto his bed. Now that the immediate danger had passed, his mind had lost its stillness and was urgently searching for a way out of the dilemma. Take Miriam out of the equation he thought, and their whole world would fall down like a pack of cards. *Their* world! It suddenly dawned on him. Lizzie! This was an issue that a father and mother would normally discuss. Really they were a family - a strange, artificial family true, but a family nevertheless.

As quietly as he could, he squeaked his wheel chair down the passage, and knocked softly on Lizzie's door. She opened it, hairbrush in hand, with her long black hair tumbling over her shoulders. She wore a dressing gown that fitted tightly around her hips and breasts; breasts that went unnoticed in the baggy uniform that he insisted she wore when working in the house. Bruno's eyes scanned the attractive figure in front of him quickly, and then closed his mind to it.

"Lizzie, we need to talk urgently. Please come to the veranda as soon as you are dressed."

Lizzie was out on the veranda within minutes. A strand of her hair, tied up in a hurry, had broken free, and was tumbling over her left cheek. She sat down on the chair Bruno had managed to pull close to his wheelchair with his foot. Without preparing her for the news, his voice a whisper, he burst out:

"Miriam's mother has showed up at the de Wits."

Anxiously he watched her eyes go wide as her skin paled against the black hair hanging on her face.

"Miriam's mother! But…"

He knew she was going to say 'but I'm her mother', and had stopped herself. It was as if their minds had locked together, and thoughts were flowing freely between them, completely transparent.

When she spoke again she sounded defiant. "Can she prove it?"

"Good point! She'd have to prove it first."

"First? You mean... You mean Miriam is going to be taken away again?" Agitation distorted Lizzie's fine features and her pain cut through Bruno's heart.

"Lizzie, please don't upset yourself." Bruno was groping for words to calm her fears – and his own. "This woman, she's a total stranger to Miriam. She won't just be whisked out of our lives. Social Services will have to check out many things: perhaps she's a drunk; I mean why did she abandon her child in the first instance? How do we know she's reliable? Can she give her a good home and education? Many, many other things that the law would require."

Lizzie put her hands to her face.

"Oh Mr. Mynhard, if she *is* Miriam's mother, if Miriam wants to go to her, can we let a law stop her?"

Bruno took a deep breath. He was desperate to convince himself and Lizzie, that their world was safe.

"What makes you think Miriam would want to go to her? Turn her back on you, whom all these years she loved as if you were her own mother? What makes you think she would trust a woman who put a helpless baby on a doorstep? Just because she's her birth mother! That's if she is. I can't see any reason why Miriam would just decide to go with her, even if the law said it was OK."

Bruno had exhausted himself. He stopped talking and sat head down, trembling slightly. Cinnamon started thumping her tail where she lay on the veranda floor, ears standing erect. Miriam must be on her way. Lizzie got up quickly. She disappeared around the corner and went through the back door into the kitchen.

For two days after their conversation, Lizzie was fighting the darkness. That familiar depression that made her feel as if she was slithering down into nothingness, non existence. That place where she was fourteen years ago, that place in her that the sun and the mountain and her youth had managed to rescue her from. She felt as if the depression had already slipped past the one she was in some months ago. Now it was heading straight for the dungeons where it was dark and dank, and this time she knew she wouldn't have the strength to claw her way out of it again.

Miriam's mother! How could she compete with her for Miriam's love? Even though Mr. Mynhard said Miriam loved her as if she was her own mother, and all the other legal stuff that would keep Miriam with her, she knew that the law and love don't necessarily go together. Legally she was still Joshua's wife, but without love everything collapsed into misery. She had already started coughing, and her chest was tightening around her heart. She knew the signs of bronchitis. Tomorrow Miriam would have to get her own and Mr. Mynhard's breakfast. She could no longer go on.

She passed the night in feverish dreams, talking to her mother, who looked pale faced.

"They want to take my baby from me again Mama!"

"No one belongs to you Lizzie, not even your children."

Lizzie started sobbing in her sleep, until her mother's voice penetrated her confused mind again.

"You'll have to bring this thing between you and Joshua to an end now."

"No!" she shouted, "I never want to set eyes on him again."

"He'll live inside you until you forgive him."

"No! No! No!"

She awoke from someone shaking her shoulder.

"Aunty Lizzie, Aunty Lizzie, wake up, you're having a nightmare!"

Miriam's concerned face was hovering over hers. She placed a cool little hand on her forehead. "You're ill, you've got a temperature. I'll get some Paracetamol and iced water."

She loves me, Lizzie said to herself. *Perhaps she'll still have a place for me in her heart after her mother had claimed her.*

CHAPTER 6

Miriam had taken charge of the housework. It was easy for her, and what with the half-term break, she breezed through her tasks. Just after ten o'clock she decided to take the dogs for a walk. There was a heavy air hanging in the house with Mr. Bruno spending long periods in his room talking on the phone which he had taken in there. His frown sat deep in his brooding face, and Aunty Lizzie drifted in and out of sleep. The doctor had been, and had prescribed an anti-biotic, and bed rest. The atmosphere felt stifling, yet at the same time she was less tied to Mr. Bruno's rules. There was nothing else for her to do now until she had to prepare lunch.

They walked down the azalea-lined driveway, and onto the dirt track leading to the main road. Halfway down the dogs stopped short and started barking, looking into the veld, but Miriam couldn't see anything. Then suddenly a braided, beaded head popped up out of the long grass with a woman pulling her pants up hastily. Immediately the dogs were on guard and started to give chase, but Miriam called them back.

"Cinnamon! Honey! Heel! Heel!"

They came back and sat in front of her growling. The hair on Cinnamon's back stood on end; just like the day they encountered the snake.

"Good morning," Miriam said.

The woman moved slowly out of the long grass, coming towards her, looking at her intently.

"Can I help you?" Miriam said when the woman stood in front of her, yet far enough away to be out of reach of the snarling dogs.

At last the woman spoke.

"I'm looking for my child, the baby I left on the doorstep of the white people. They told me she lives on this side of the mountain now."

As if the mountain went into shock, the shadows from the high cliffs, throwing themselves into the abyss below, seemed to shudder. Or was it the movement of the white eagle suddenly taking off from some hidden perch that made it look like that? The eagle swooped low; it's shrieks echoing through the valley. Miriam stood stony still, only her eyes moving between the snakeskin handbag and the woman's face.

"You are that baby, aren't you? Aren't you my love?"

Miriam felt a peculiar sensation rising slowly from her gut, up and up her body, until it got stuck in her throat, preventing her from speaking.

The woman edged nearer with outstretched arm, trying to touch her, but the dogs were now barking uncontrollably, and Cinnamon was whining with exasperation in between the barks. The woman stepped back.

"I've come to fetch you my darling. Oh how I've longed for you all these years! I've got a good home to take you to in Johannesburg. Oh, I love you so much."

Suddenly the lump that was stuck in Miriam's throat dislodged itself and started to pour out of her in the form of a deep long sigh. When the sigh stopped, the words tumbled out:

"Then why did you give me away? Why did you abandon me on strange people's doorstep? Like a stray dog!!"

Miriam didn't recognize her own voice. It sounded swollen, like the flesh around a wound that was oozing pus. She took a deep breath and opened her mouth again to say more but she felt empty, exhausted. There was nothing more to say. She closed her mouth again as her eyes searched for the eagle, which was hovering just above the high cliffs, balancing itself gracefully in the still air.

There was a vibration on the dirt track and she recognized the sound of a motorcar. Cinnamon stopped whining and pricked up her ears. Miriam saw Sunda and

Abdullah's blue Buick as it wound its way up the narrow dirt track. Abdullah stopped next to Miriam.

"Come to see how your Aunty Lizzie is. Mr. Mynhard phoned to say you couldn't come over because she's ill."

He looked at the woman clutching her handbag nervously, and nodded his head in greeting. The dogs had gathered around the car now, wagging their tails, and thump, thumping them against the car doors. The woman took courage and came closer, and the dogs let her. Abdullah looked questioningly at Miriam. The lump was in her throat again, but she managed to squeeze out:

"She's… she says she's my mother."

"Your mother!" Abdullah and Sunda's voices were like one.

Miriam nodded. Abdullah switched the engine off and got out of the car.

"You're Miriam's mother?"

The woman smiled for the first time and Miriam saw the orange-pink of false teeth, slightly loose, in her mouth.

"Is that the name they've given her, my darling daughter? Miriam." She looked affectionately at Miriam.

"Where do you live, eh…?"

"Hester."

"Where do you live Hester?"

"In Johannesburg."

"Ah, I know Johannesburg, lived there a good number of years myself, which part?"

The woman's eyes grew cautious.

"Parktown. I've got a house there. I can take Miriam home now."

"Parktown! Oh you must be well off then. Did you drive all the way to the Berg yourself? Where's your car?"

The woman was beginning to look very uncomfortable.

"I came with the train."

"The train! That's a hell of a journey. How many different trains did you have to take from Durban to here?"

The woman seemed flustered fiddling with her handbag

"I came with the taxi."

94

"Jesus, taxi from Durban to the Berg! You're sure a wealthy lady."

Abdullah opened the back door.

"Well get in Hester, I'll take you up to the house to fetch Miriam's clothes. Miriam, you go on with the dogs, and we'll see you up there later."

As the woman got into the car he gave Miriam a broad wink and mouthed 'don't worry'.

Just inside Bruno's driveway he suddenly stopped the car, locked the doors and pulled the ignition key out. Then he turned to the woman.

"Which pimp do you work for? Where is he waiting for you?"

The woman's face turned ashen grey.

"What are you talking about? Miriam is my child, I've come to fetch her home."

"And how are you going to prove she's yours?"

"Well how would I have known about her if she wasn't mine?"

Abdullah snorted. "How much is he paying you for this?"

"Unlock my door Abdullah," Sunda said, "I'll go ahead and warn Mr. Mynhard so that he can get the police."

The woman became hysterical and started banging against the windows.

"Let me out! Let me out! I'm an innocent mother coming for my child!"

"What did he say he'll do to you if you come back empty handed?" Abdullah's voice was kind now, and the woman broke down. Sunda turned around and put a consoling hand on her leg.

"Better to tell the truth Hester, that way you don't get into double trouble. You see Miriam has got foster parents; even if you were her mother you couldn't just take her away. Social Services will check it out first."

The woman sat hunched up sobbing for a while, then,

"I told him it wouldn't be that easy. I said, *why bother with a child*? But all he kept saying was: *lambs meat, that's what those kind of men want - lambs meat*".

"How did you know about Miriam?" Sunda repeated Hester's question of a minute ago."

The woman blew her nose loudly and sat staring out of the window.

"She's a beautiful girl this Miriam, her mother would have been proud of her."

"Would have been?"

She turned aggressively towards Sunda. "This is none of your business. I'll tell the *girl*. She's the one who's to know."

Abdullah started the car up again.

"If we explain to Mr. Mynhard, I'm sure he wouldn't lay a charge. He'll let you tell Miriam."

As the car drove off with Hester in the back Miriam stood shock-glued in the dust kicked up by the car, burning her throat and irritating her eyes. She had the strangest feeling in her chest and it seemed to spread, engulfing her whole torso, her legs, her arms and head. This amazing feeling of lightness in her body! As if something oppressive, heavy, had left her. She thought of the lump that was stuck in her throat and how empty she had felt after she asked this woman, who was pretending to be her mother, why she had abandoned her, and had shouted out the words: "Like a stray dog!"

Her body swayed from side to side, and for a moment she did not quite know where she was until Honey nudged her for an ear cuddle and Cinnamon circled around her, impatient to continue the walk.

The strange moment passed and she took hold of herself. She felt the gentlest of breeze stroking her hair and it seemed to her that the mountain, that solid mass of rock, had steadied her. She looked up into the sky – the eagle had gone, but the bird song that filled the air seemed exquisitely beautiful to her. She stood listening to it for a moment, and then turned to the dogs.

"Come on Cinnamon, Honey, we're going back home, no more walks today."

The dogs followed, reluctant to be moving into the direction they've just come from and Cinnamon veered off the path every now and again disappearing into the long grass, just to get as much of a run as possible out of the aborted walk.

The first thing that Miriam saw when she reached the house was that Aunty Lizzie was out of bed, sitting in her dressing gown on the veranda with the others, looking grey as a corpse. Hester was sitting upright on the veranda bench all by herself, facing the other four. Mr. Bruno was saying:

"Miriam has the right to know the whereabouts of her mother."

Sunda and Abdullah nodded their heads. Aunty Lizzie started that awful cough again and it sounded like she was in great pain. Mr. Bruno looked at Abdullah.

"Shall we agree then that they talk in private?"

Abdullah nodded again. "That will be the best way." He turned to Hester. "But how will we know that you will tell her the truth?"

Hester jerked her head angrily. "Ag shit man, how will I know you won't set the police on me after I've told her."

Abdullah laughed. "You won't know." The dogs were on the veranda now, wagging their tails, and everyone became aware of Miriam's puzzled face. He pointed to Miriam. "But Miriam here, she will know if what comes out of your mouth is the truth. She's got second sight, she sees things."

Miriam's jaw dropped, but she quickly regained her composure when she looked into Abdullah's liquid brown eyes. He gave her a slight, almost imperceptible, wink.

Hester looked at Miriam in awe. "Jesus! Like her mother!"

Mr. Bruno said, "Miriam, take Hester to your room", and to Hester: "There will be no trouble if you tell her the truth."

Miriam gave Hester the easy chair and sat on the upright one. Hester looked out of the window for a while, a sadness surrounding her whole being. At last she spoke:

"Your mother is dead."

To Miriam this came not so much as a shock, more as a confirmation of some vague feeling she has had for some time now deep inside her. She wanted to ask Hester when she died and how, but Hester had already started to talk again.

"Your mother was kitchen girl for the white people who lived in a big house in Parktown. I worked next door. Our off times we sat together on the pavements in the sun. I asked your mother why she never bought herself new clothes, or went to the movies. She told me about you. She said she put you at the door of the house of the boss of the orphanage, because people said he was a kind man, and she wanted for you to live and grow up strong. She was saving her money so that one day she could buy a house and go fetch you."

Something melted in Miriam like soft butter, and spread all over her stomach. She knew Hester was telling the truth.

"And my father, did she ever talk about him? Did she tell you what he looked like?"

"Yes", she said, "he was a painter, he'd come from far away to paint *this* beautiful mountain" There was a longing in her voice.

"What did he look like?"

"How can I know, I never saw him, may be he had green eyes like yours."

"What did my mother look like?"

Hester sighed. "She was so slim, she was only seventeen when she came to work at that house in Parktown."

"Yes, but what did she look like; her hair, her eyes, her face?"

"Her hair looked just like all Zulu's hair, not like yours that can grow into nice frizzy curls." She paused and sat staring out in front or her. "Her eyes were so gentle, and they always smiled when her face was smiling. It was nice to be with her. I thought perhaps her daughter might be like her, may be come and live with me." There was a longing in her voice as she looked at Miriam. "He painted a picture of her."

"A picture! Did you see it?"

"No, she said he took it with him, he said he wanted to remember her by it."

Then Miriam asked the big question. "What was her name?"

Hester shrugged. "I don't know her Zulu name. We all take white people's names when we come to work for them. The name she told to them was Lokkie."

"Lokkie," Miriam rolled the name around her tongue. "Lokkie."

"Yes, Lokkie," Hester said. "Lokkie who saved all her money, the pittance the white people paid us; to buy a house." Hester's voice was bitter now. "A house on a kitchen girl's wages. She didn't see that the best you could do with that money was to buy a new dress, go to the movies, and get drunk whenever the sorrow wants to kill you. She kept every month's money in a tin under her bed, never thought anyone would steal her money."

Miriam's heart sank, and she could feel the fear setting her chest into an uneven spin.

"How did she die?"

Hester looked at her, fierce anger in her eyes.

"They broke into her room the bastards! And they killed her because she fought them for that tin of money: two year's money."

"How do you know that was how it happened Hester?"

"Ag, it's easy man, two days later the gardener at the end of the road swanked a new coat, and it wasn't even pay day yet. We all knew he got pissed on the last pay day; all his money gone. And the other bastard, suddenly he had money for a taxi to Benoni, to go see his family with arms full of presents; and the master of the house, he found no money in her room. Just her – killed! She knew them, they knew she could tell the police."

Miriam sat lost in the vision of a young girl bravely defending her tin of money against two robbers. Her mother. The money she had saved for her. She started crying. But Hester sat motionless, the corners of her mouth drawn down, a bitter woman.

"After Lokkie was murdered," she continued as if she'd forgotten about this innocent young girl sitting in front of her, "I just said fuck you to earning pittance and went onto the streets, the pimp offered more, *and* protection. Protection! Ha. What protection when he forced me after I got drunk one night and told him Lokkie's story? And look at me now sitting deep in the shit. "

Miriam didn't know what she meant, but the way her face looked then, she was too scared to ask. Hester had suddenly changed, and the image of her coming out of the long grass after she had relieved herself flashed through her mind. She didn't want to hear her mother's name coming out of this woman's mouth again. She didn't want to be with her any more. She felt raw inside and longed for Aunty Lizzie. She got up and said:

"Thank you Hester. I know you've told me the truth. I will tell Mr. Mynhard so."

It was as if Hester came out of the world into which she had just sunk and looked at Miriam, eyes wide.

"Eh, you truly have got second sight just like your mother. For sure your mother knew she was going to die that night when she said to me: *If I die before I have fetched my baby, my spirit will go to her whenever trouble comes for her. My love will help her.*"

Miriam's legs gave way under her and she knew nothing more until she saw Aunty Lizzie and Sunda's faces hovering above her, calling her name.

Bruno decided to buy Miriam her own computer: he never liked anyone using his, and he could no longer keep up with her insatiable thirst for knowledge. Questions, questions, questions - he couldn't possibly work out lessons on all the areas of her interest. But he was also very concerned that she wasn't to get drawn into the world of computer games, and, God forbid, social media! Who knew what might happen then? He also felt strongly that she shouldn't have access to email – she could be 'talking' to anyone, and they would never know. No, the computer was to be strictly for the use of gathering information for essays on topics, which they would agree to beforehand. He would make that clear to her - and outside of those times her laptop was to be locked up with his own in the computer desk.

He was thinking of how much she had changed since that woman from Johannesburg had been here. She didn't act like the thirteen, fourteen year olds he knew at school, but much more like an adult – and her insights into situations were sharp and wise. She had also become secretive. Even Lizzie couldn't get anything out of her about what Hester had told her. All she was willing to say was:

"My mother is dead."

"How did she die?" Lizzie had asked.

"Murdered." Just the one word, nothing more.

"No wonder she fainted," Lizzie had said to him afterwards, and they decided not to press her for more information, though judging from the time the woman had been with her, much more than just that must have been said. But he had always been one for respecting people's privacy. In any case, for him, the fact that Miriam's mother was no longer alive was the best possible outcome to the whole situation. Everything was going his way. He now regarded Lizzie, Miriam, and himself as a family. A happy family.

He decided that Ben would be the best person to advise him on a suitable laptop for Miriam. There was talk of him coming up for Easter, so he could bring it up with him.

He smiled to himself. All was well.

When Bruno told Miriam that Ben was coming and bringing her a laptop, she felt as if she'd grown wings, and could fly with her eagle high up in the sky. The laptop was a small part of her joy. She was going to see Ben again!

Aunty Lizzie asked her to clean the outside spare room, now mainly used as a storeroom. "We'll get Filamon to open up one of the fold-up beds and then you can make it up for Ben."

"What about his girlfriend? Is she not coming?"

"No, Mr. Mynhard said they've split up."

Miriam's heart was singing and she counted the days to Easter. It felt like years since she had last seen him. She was thirteen now, with breasts puffing out the front of her dress. Would Ben notice?

Long before she could hear Ben's car coming, Cinnamon's ears told her that he was near, and Honey got up heavily to contribute a few half-hearted barks to the arrival. She had gone so fat lately and slept most of the time when they were not out walking. The dogs were the first to meet him, but she was not far behind.

"Miriam! He hugged her then held her at arms length.

"Let me look at you."

She could see that he had noticed her breasts. She blushed.

"Growing into the beauty of the year, hey?" He gave her cheek a few playful strokes.

Her heart felt so big she thought it could contain the whole mountain.

Mr. Bruno squeaked out in his wheelchair, and Ben went over to greet him.

"Dad, good to see you, you look well!"

Aunty Lizzie was out on the veranda now.

"And this must be the famous Lizzie," he said. "No doubt the reason why you look so well cared for Dad." Ben shook hands with Aunty Lizzie. "So please to meet you," and then on impulse he hugged her too.

Everyone was happy, even Honey seemed to have more life in her, wagging her tail energetically.

That evening at supper Ben asked a lot about Miriam's paintings and then:

"Have you done one of yourself perhaps?"

"Ah no," she said feeling awkward.

Ben also talked to Aunty Lizzie a lot, and Miriam could see she was really enjoying it. But when he started asking her questions about where she lived in Cape Town she clammed up, answering just the bare minimum. Ben asked no more, but looked at her with a strange interest in his eyes. It set Miriam thinking about Aunty Lizzie's past. She had never thought of her as having had a life of her own before she was born. She seemed to have been there for her always.

The following morning Ben set Miriam's laptop up and showed her how to work it. She sat next to Ben, and could smell him. Not his after-shave lotion, no, him, his... well, his what? She didn't know, only knew this was how Ben smelled, and no one else could smell like that, not Abdullah, not Mr. Bruno, no one else, just Ben.

Mr. Bruno had reluctantly agreed to Ben's request to waive the last school day's lessons before the Easter break, so that she could learn about the laptop.

"I guess it can be counted as education," he muttered grudgingly.

"Of course dad, it's part of the curriculum in schools these days."

Mr. Bruno didn't like *that*; his frown became long again. But still she had to go for her rest after lunch. She was furious. She didn't want Ben to see her anger in case he didn't like her any more, but she closed her bedroom door with a bang. There was no question of her resting, let alone sleeping. She took a book and tried to read, but concentrating was out of the question. Ben was out there and she could have been talking to him now, without Mr. Bruno trying to control the conversation. She was thrashing around on her bed, angry thoughts rushing through her head all directed at 'that man with his long frown'.

In the end she decided it was no use lying there and got up quietly to choose the dress she was going to wear for Easter Sunday when Abdullah and Sunda were coming over to meet Ben. The curtains of her bedroom window were open and that was when she saw them: Ben and Aunty Lizzie coming slowly up the gravel path, apparently back from a walk – all by themselves! They didn't even have the dogs with them! They were deep in conversation, totally absorbed in it; and then Miriam saw Ben put his arm around Aunty Lizzie's shoulder and gave it a little squeeze.

She felt as if she could die. *How dare he touch my Aunty Lizzie! She belongs to me! And Aunty Lizzie, how dare she... well, what?* Everything inside her was in a muddle. Her thoughts were racing: *I'm the one who should be walking and talking with Ben, touched by him, admired by him! Not Aunty Lizzie! How could she! How could he!* Her heart felt as if it had split into two, Ben had one half, and Aunty Lizzie had the other. She felt like trashing her room to pieces. She fell back on her bed, and buried her head in the bedclothes to smother her sobs. She felt abandoned, betrayed. How could they! She sobbed and sobbed until she felt totally empty.

It was then that the voice came; and it dropped just two words into her mind like pebbles into a pond: *Jealousy and possessiveness*, and then the ripples from the pebbles said: *Nobody belongs to you.*

Unlike in the past, the voice didn't console her; rather it chastised her: but in a strange way she was glad for it, because she knew then that neither Aunty Lizzie, nor Ben could stop the coming of the voice. It belonged to her, and her alone. She would always keep it a secret from them.

She dried her eyes, combed her hair, and when her time for resting was over, went outside to take the dogs for their walk.

Bruno had started to feel uncomfortable at supper the night before when he noticed the dance of joy that twirled between Ben and Lizzie. He saw Ben's eyes light up when he scanned Lizzie's figure as she got up from the table to serve the dessert, dressed, not in her uniform but, in a pretty dress. The gall rose up in him and his mind started down a well-worn path: *whenever he comes to visit he upsets things.* It has always been like that, even when he was a boy; and he often upset Amelie too. He's just like his mother, the same probing into people's feelings, like a sniffer dog. How dare he ask Lizzie all those questions about herself? She had confided in him, about her dead baby, and it had nothing to do with Ben who only came to visit when he needed something. *Wonder what he wants this time?*

The next morning Bruno felt grumpy, and having his usual routine interrupted by computer lessons didn't help things. He clung to what authority he had left, and insisted that Miriam went for her rest. But *he* couldn't rest: he sat staring out of his window, and that was when he saw Ben and Lizzie setting off on their walk. They didn't even have the excuse of taking the dogs for a walk, because it wasn't the dog's time for walking. Even they knew that, and stayed obediently in their baskets.

Sitting there, a long forgotten feeling jumped up from the depth of his being, of how idyllic his life was as a little boy with his mother and grandmother before his father returned from the war. The thought of how his arrival had destroyed that, brought up all the old wounds, and his anger raced towards Ben. *He's barging into my home and upsetting the sweetness of my life with Miriam and Lizzie - just like that man did!*

After what seemed to him like an eternity he saw them coming back, and he saw what Miriam saw, and he saw his father putting his arm around his mother's shoulders; and he, the little boy Bruno, was being made to rest, while they were cavorting in the garden, laughing and talking. He felt excluded, he felt abandoned by his mother; and he hated this ex-soldier. He wanted to thrash the living daylights out of him, but knew he couldn't. He could only watch, paralysed with anger.

And now he couldn't beat Ben up either, because he was paralysed.

A wave of resentment flowed over him. Ben always seemed to bring the past up for him; a past that he had wanted to forget at all costs.

Lizzie was surprised at the feelings of joy that surfaced in her at Ben's attentions. Men, to her mind, were in a category that was best left alone. Love was associated with children. Miriam. But from Ben, she felt something that was very pleasing: respectful acknowledgement of her womanhood.

And so it was that when Ben asked her to go with him for a little walk, she felt safe, and her defences dropped away as they were both admiring the fullness of the autumn colours.

"When I left Cape Town the trees were nearly bare, because of the high winds, as you well know," Ben said in his undemanding voice, and Lizzie felt herself transported to many Cape scenes. Nostalgia filled her heart, an emotion the luxury of which she had not allowed herself for years.

"Ah, I can just see that beautiful place." There was such a longing in her voice that it was inevitable that Ben would ask.

"What made you leave the Cape for this lonely place?" and Lizzie heard herself say:

"I fled from my past."

"A painful past, by the sound of your voice."

Ben's voice was stroking, and the last of Lizzie's defences crumbled. It was easier than she thought it would be to talk about Joshua and the stillborn baby. Afterwards she felt light, and they walked in silence to the end of the path where it joined up with the main road. When they turned back, Ben asked:

"So you're still married to Joshua then?"

She nodded.

"Do you still want to be married to him?"

"Of course not! I never, ever want to see him again!" Lizzie heard her voice coming as from afar, and it sounded harsh - ugly.

"You hate him that much?"

She nodded as the tears started to roll across her cheeks. Ben led her to a flat stone by the edge of the road.

"Let's sit down." After a while: "So you're married to a man you hate and to whom you don't want to be married?"

Lizzie tilted her head vigorously. "He doesn't exist for me any more!"

"Oh but he does Lizzie, he lives inside you, within that hatred you feel for him."

Lizzie was sobbing now, her hand holding her little handkerchief clenched into a fist. "He killed my baby! I could kill him, I could kick his head into pulp!"

"Is that what you're afraid of Lizzie? Is that why you don't want to see him again?"

Lizzie stopped sobbing and looked at Ben, startled. Then slowly she wiped her tears and blew her nose. After a while they got up and continued their walk. Neither of them said anymore, until they were in sight of the house. Then Ben said:

"If you want Joshua out of your life Lizzie, you're going to have to face those feelings inside yourself."

"But how?" Lizzie protested. "How? I can never forgive him. He killed my child, for God's sake!"

Ben put a consoling arm around her.

"You're a wise women Lizzie, you'll find a way in your own time," and he gave her shoulders a little squeeze.

He called me a wise woman, Lizzie thought. *No one has ever called me that.*

Lizzie thought of the time when Miriam was beginning to lose her faith in her rock God, and she, herself, was doubting that benevolent Presence whom she believed had given Miriam to her, and who now, a second time, had allowed her to keep Miriam. Perhaps that Presence was speaking to her through Ben, and through dreams. Perhaps it would come to her aid again.

Bruno's anger was bursting at the seams when he rode out to inspect Filamon's work. At the hen pen, the red hen stuck her head through the still not mended hole, cocked it, and surveyed Bruno with a beady eye.

"Filamon!" Bruno's voice thundered around the smallholding with great ferocity.

Ben and Lizzie felt, more than heard, the angry vibrations galloping around the house. Lizzie was taking the washing off the line, and was lingering in the sunshine as long as possible, contemplating her conversation with Ben. But now she nervously stuffed the washing into the blue bowl, and carried it into the laundry that stood aside from the house. Closing the door, she started on the ironing.

Ben was in the house, about to switch the TV on, but instinctively felt that when his dad came in and saw the TV on at that time of the day, it would be like a red rag to a bull. He took a book from the shelf instead and tried to read. When he came to the end of the page he had no sense of what he had been reading. He knew he had been in that place inside himself before, and that he didn't want to be there. The last time he had experienced those feelings was when his mother ended up with a broken arm, and his whole life changed. And just like then, he felt anger coming from everywhere in the house. It was as if the enormity of his father's anger, contained in just that one word: *Filamon*, had magically transformed him into a frightened little boy again. He was standing helpless before a memory that refused to fade.

Both Ben and Lizzie listened in awe to the loud tongue lashing that Filamon was getting before Bruno's wheelchair hissed into the lounge.

"Where's Lizzie?"

"I don't know Dad, she's probably seeing to the washing." Ben tried to keep his voice from trembling.

"I would have thought she'd finished with that long ago."

Ben said nothing and kept his eyes on the book he was trying to read.

Bruno turned his wheelchair around fiercely and made straight for the laundry.

"Lizzie! Lizzie, are you in there?"

Lizzie opened the door.

"Yes Mr. Mynhard, just doing the ironing."

"That should have been done long ago, you should be preparing supper by now."

Lizzie held the iron close to her chest as if in defence. What she saw in front of her was not Bruno, but Joshua, coming to beat her up.

"Nearly finished Mr. Mynhard, coming right away."

Bruno said nothing more when Lizzie closed the door on him quickly and he heard her lock it. He hesitated a moment then steered himself to the veranda. There he sat for a long time staring at the marble hand, which looked to him as if it was begging for mercy, until he heard Miriam calling to the dogs.

They came onto the veranda, Cinnamon first, with Honey huffing and puffing behind her. But Miriam had already seen Bruno staring at the hand from the garden, and that he was wearing the deepest frown she had ever seen, which looked dark in the fading light. Instinctively she sensed his anger as it resonated with her own resentment.

She pulled a chair up next to his and they sat in silence for a while; then:

"Honey is getting old Mr. Bruno, and she's far too fat."

He nodded.

On impulse Miriam took his lame hand in both hers and started massaging it gently. Bruno let out a long sigh, and then his shoulders shook. She kept on massaging the hand, stroking it at intervals. Dusk was falling fast now, and slowly the enormous mountain that was there a while ago disappeared, giving over to a starlit sky. They sat together, listening to the crickets until Lizzie announced that supper was ready.

A gloomy atmosphere surrounded the four of them as they sat around the dining table, each absorbed in their own unhappy thoughts:

Ben became aware that he was sitting with his shoulders hunched up as if he was about to pull his head into his torso, like a tortoise. The fear was playing havoc in his chest, an almost overwhelming emotion. Yet at the same time a part of him was somehow able to stand back from it, watching. He was now neither the cocky schoolboy, defying his father just because he knew the man could do nothing about it any more, nor the psychologist analysing his own feelings. He was simply Ben the frightened little boy. He felt very vulnerable sitting there, looking across the table at his father, whose face was a dark cloud, his lame hand resting on the table beside his plate.

Lizzie picked at her food. She had no appetite. Every time she looked at Mr. Mynhard, she saw Joshua, and her impulse was to leave this place as soon as possible. But she was trapped: leave and she would lose Miriam, stay, and she would have to face the anger she'd been running away from for years now. Ben said Joshua lived within her, inside her own hatred for him. So what good would leaving do? She felt helpless.

Bruno sat brooding, still very angry, but he was beginning to feel in control. He looked from his lame hand to Miriam who sat alert, eyes darting to and fro between Ben and Lizzie. Without knowing why, he sensed that he had an ally in her.

Miriam was observing Ben and Lizzie with a strange detachment that she'd not experienced before. She still felt jealous, she still felt piqued, but in a deep down place inside herself, a place that she was barely aware off, she had understood the meaning of what the voice had said: that neither of them belonged to her. Only the voice inside her belonged to her, or she to it. But who or what was this voice? Could this then be the true God? She did not know. It was all far too complicated. It was easier to think about what her eyes could see at that moment: the incredible vulnerability in both Ben and Aunty Lizzie. Aunty Lizzie, the strong woman who had always been there for her through out her childhood years, suddenly looked scared and very insecure. She'd never seen her like that before, and she felt like her world had suddenly expanded to take in other, hitherto hidden, realities.

And Ben, oh how she would love to paint him just as he looked right then: with the eyes of a child, vulnerable and confused. She did not have to look at Mr. Bruno. Instinctively she was beginning to understand his pain, his longings, the games he played - his need for her. It made her bold.

"Ben," she said, "I must make a picture of you. Mr. Bruno, please, tomorrow is Good Friday; may I spend the day painting Ben?"

"But you've already made a picture of Ben, Miriam" Bruno said, his frown folding away.

"Oh but that was of a different Ben!"

"How do you mean a different me?" Ben asked, the psychologist's interest aroused.

"You'll see when you look into your eyes in the picture," was all Miriam would say. "Is that OK Mr. Bruno?"

Bruno's acute fear of losing, to Ben, the closeness he felt he had with Lizzie, was relieved by the thought that letting Miriam paint Ben, would keep him away from her. Besides, he couldn't afford to have Miriam against him while Ben was here.

"Yes, fine with me, if it is OK with Ben."

Ben relaxed. He was the adult again. "Of course, I'd be honoured."

"Lizzie," Bruno said, trying to make amends, "that was an excellent meal. How about that pudding of yours now?" He turned to Ben. "Lizzie makes a bread and butter pudding the calibre of which I'd last tasted in your grandmother's home."

Lizzie smiled and got up. She had left Joshua's home, and was back in the Berg bringing up Miriam and making a home for her.

CHAPTER 7

Painting Ben this time took Miriam much longer than just Good Friday; it gobbled up Saturday too, still leaving work to be done around the eyes. Miriam wasn't quite sure why it took her longer than she had anticipated. Was it to extend her time in Ben's company, or to keep him away from Aunty Lizzie, or both? Or did it just take longer than she thought to get that frightened little boy look in his eyes right, now that he was no longer frightened?

On Sunday afternoon Sunda and Abdullah visited and brought the spices Bruno had ordered as well as his post. Abdullah held a letter out to a surprised Lizzie. It was addressed to her c/o Mrs. Evan's address in Durban and readdressed c/o Mr. De Wit, from where it was forwarded to Bruno's post box. With a shock Lizzie recognised her father's large, all-over-the-place, scribble and her legs started to wobble. He hardly ever wrote letters. This could mean only one thing. She took the letter and went to her room.

The first thing she noticed when she opened it was the Cape Town address at the top, with the name of a suburb unfamiliar to her. It was written on two pages torn from an exercise book and started with a salute: '*Hallelujah!! God bless you my dear Lizzie. God bless your dear mother, she is not long for this world. Any day now. The cancer has got her. Please come home, she wants to see you. We live in our own nice house now, just the three of us. Samuel he is with the army and Bennet he gone to England. Sarah is looking after your mother, God bless her. Hallelujah!*

Our own house he says, do they own it? Surely not! Lizzie's thoughts were in turmoil. She read on but there wasn't much more information just some more Hallelujahs and God Blessings, and plenty of smear marks.

So this is it, Lizzie thought, *I have to go to Cape Town.* Her spine was shaking and she held on to the bedstead. *Joshua, will he still be living there? What if I bump into him?* The very thought made her feel sick and she rushed to the toilet, just in time. She felt totally trapped; how could she refuse her mother's dying wish? She had to go, and as Ben said, face Joshua, but deep down inside her she held onto the hope that he might not be in Cape Town any more, that she might not encounter him at all. She washed her face, combed her hair and went out to the others on the veranda.

"Mr. Mynhard," her voice was wobbly, "The letter was from my father, my mother is dying in Cape Town."

She caught Ben's eyes from the corner of hers and somehow felt strength coming towards her. She didn't notice the fright on Bruno's face, or the shock on Miriam's.

Ben got up and took Lizzie's hands in his. "Lizzie I'm so sorry."

"Yes of course!" Bruno croaked, and the others chimed in.

"I can give you a lift down Lizzie," Ben's voice was full of compassion.

"It seems she might have only days to live," Lizzie's voice was firmer now.

"It might be best then if we leave straight away. We will have to travel through the night, but could be there by late tomorrow afternoon."

Miriam had heard the relief in Ben's voice when he said 'leave straight away' and her disappointment mingled with anguish. She wanted to show the finished painting to Ben, hear his appreciation and praise, but fate had now thrown Aunty Lizzie and Ben together again! Her stomach churned, and as she looked across to Mr. Bruno and saw his face darken, it dawned on her that they feared the same unspeakable thing.

Lizzie's motherly concern was not dampened by the news.

"But how can Miriam cope alone? She's got her studies, and Katrina can't come back now that she's got that job with the Oberolzers."

"I will get extra help in," Bruno said, "there's plenty of people looking for work. Miriam only needs to show them the ways we want things done here."

Ben and Lizzie packed quickly, and when Bruno assured her again that there was no need to worry about Miriam, she was ready to go.

When they said goodbye, Bruno looked intently at Lizzie.

"You will come back, won't you Lizzie?"

Lizzie's eyes widened in amazement, "But of course I will Mr. Mynhard, *you* know that."

Bruno cast his eyes down before the honesty in Lizzie's face and felt ashamed at his sudden panicking, especially as he recalled their intimate conversation about what Miriam meant to her - to both of them.

Ben gave Miriam a warm brotherly hug. "Will you be able to finish the picture without me now?" he asked.

"Yes", she replied, as she scanned the shape of his eyes again, "yes I will, from memory."

As they drove off Bruno and Miriam stood watching the car until it hit the dirt road obscuring it from view by the swirling dust.

After Ben and Lizzie had left, and the days passed, Bruno gradually became aware of a subtle shift in the relationship between him and Miriam and his feelings towards her. He was beginning to view her less as a child, almost as a companion. He let her sit in when he interviewed girls to temporarily help out with the housework and they discussed it afterwards.

"I think Maria would be the best one Mr. Bruno"

"She's a bit young I think, only fifteen." Bruno was looking at the list of names in front of him.

"But she's got eyes that laugh and I like the sound of her voice."

Bruno looked at Miriam in astonishment. "You don't miss much, do you?" he said, feeling slightly uncomfortable.

Miriam said nothing. Then... "It would be kind of company for me Mr. Bruno. Katrina never smiled and we could hardly speak to each other with the little English she knew. With Maria here I won't feel so lonely."

Guilt surfaced in Bruno: that word 'lonely' had been thrown at him before.

"O.K., we'll give her a chance. Tell Filamon to send word to Maria to start tomorrow."

For Miriam, the best part of having Maria in the house was that she sang while she worked. A firm melodious voice that rang through the house while she dusted, swept, and made the beds. But this joyful sound was very nearly quashed. Miriam and Bruno were doing their lessons on the veranda when this pleasant vibration reached their ears. Miriam's spontaneous smile coincided with Bruno's frown.

"We can't have that disturbance going on while we work! Go and tell her to be quiet."

Miriam did not move.

"I don't think it is a disturbance. I think it's beautiful."

The defiance in Miriam's voice dropped like a rock between them and sat there unmovable. Bruno felt helpless. If only Lizzie was here, he thought as he lifted his lame hand onto the table and put it near the marble hand. He saw a faint mocking smile on Miriam's face as she looked at the hand appearing on the table. He sensed no compassion for it in her now, and she continued with her map-making as if he hadn't spoken.

Bruno didn't know what to do. He was at sea without a compass. *How is it possible?* He mused. *I've been a schoolmaster and headmaster who gave orders, which were obeyed. Yet here in this lonely place with just one*

pupil, suddenly I seem to have no authority, no control!
Control - losing control? He shuddered. Slowly he moved his hand back onto his lap as a great sadness enveloped him, and he felt a slight moistness in his eyes. He couldn't get away from the truth: *I need her, and what's more, I'm developing a love for her.* Amelie sprang to his mind. He looked at the marble hand. Was it begging or receiving? Or was it begging to receive the wisdom he needed?

He thought of Ben and that first picture Miriam had made of him with the light in his eyes. How was it that he never recognized that loveliness in Ben? Not even as a baby. All he could remember was Ben absorbing all Valerie's time, altering their passionate lovemaking of those first few years before his birth. Always fresh, always new, spontaneous. He gave a deep sigh as for no reason he thought of his father.

There was a sudden insight: history repeating itself again.

He became aware that Miriam had put her pencils away and was looking at him. The clock said the geography lesson was over.

"Miriam," he asked on impulse, "have you managed to finish the latest picture of Ben yet?"

"Oh yes Mr. Bruno!" Miriam was all enthusiasm. "Would you like to see it?"

He nodded. She shot out of her chair nearly knocking it over, and rushed to her bedroom.

When she laid the picture out on the table Bruno leaned closer to it and... met Ben's frightened eyes. He gasped.

"But Ben's eyes don't look like that!"

"They did that night at the table after he and Aunty Lizzie went for that walk!"

The unspeakable thing was hovering between them.

"But why was he frightened?"

Miriam shrugged.

Bruno remembered how very angry he was that night and his inability to hide it. He also remembered his father's uncontrollable anger and his own fears of him. He put his face in his hand.

"Oh my God!"

"Miriam!" Maria was calling from the front door. "Please to come show me to cook the vegetables."

"Please excuse me Mr. Bruno," Miriam said politely before she disappeared into the house.

Bruno just sat there, holding his head in his hand. Would his father never leave him alone? What must he do to keep him in his grave once and for all!

It was after three o'clock when Ben and Lizzie hit the motorway, just outside Worcester. It was a relief after the long journey on the slower-going main road they took from Ladysmith. Another hour and they could see the Cape Flats sprawling in front of them with blobs of autumn colours breaking the monotony of concrete rows. Lizzie watched the road signs for the name of the apparent new development that was their destination. Her heart was throbbing in her throat at the sight of the familiar names: Kraaifontein, Bellville, Parrow, Goodwood. The address on the letter in her hand seemed to suggest a suburb south west of Parrow. They followed the instructions from the SatNav and before long they arrived at their destination.

Ben got out and lifted Lizzie's luggage from the boot, but when he started carrying it to the front door, she laid a hand on his arm.

"Ben, please, I need to do this by myself. Thank you so very much for bringing me to here."

Ben scanned her face for a moment, "OK". He took a card from his wallet. "Here, ring me if you need me. Promise?" He looked at her intently. "Promise?"

She nodded. "Thank you Ben," and as he got into the car a second shaky "Thank you" slipped from her mouth.

Lizzie waited until his car had disappeared around the corner before she turned around. She stood in front of a neat little house in a row of newly built dwellings, each one fenced off securely. Two houses down a dog was barking at the gate, and further down the street a black cat with white paws strutted, tail in the air, towards her. Not a dissimilar neighbourhood to the one she and Joshua had lived in she thought.

A gust of wind plucked at her light cardigan and ruffled her hair as she opened the gate and walked to the front door where she rung the bell. It was protected by a heavy iron gate. So different from their crime free life in the Berg, she thought.

It took some time before she heard some footsteps from the inside. The door opened cautiously and the first thing she recognized through the small opening was Sarah's reddish blond hair, unmistakeably hers.

"Sarah," she said, and the door opened wide, showing a full figured young women with an apron in front of her scarlet coloured dress, face all astonishment.

"Lizzie! Is that really you? Ag Heretjie tog my sussie!"*

She quickly unlocked the iron gate and flung her arms around Lizzie holding her tight as she sobbed: "I thought I'd never see my Lizzie again!" She pulled Lizzie inside and dragged the suitcase in.

Lizzie stood in the hallway breathing in the air of cleanliness and the smell of freshly baked bread while Sarah carefully locked the gate and door.

"Where is our Mama?" Lizzie asked as her eyes darted from door to door.

Sarah took a step back and stared at Lizzie. Seeing Sarah look like that, the knowingness just bubbled up in Lizzie.

"I'm too late, she's gone?"

Sarah nodded, her eyes filled to the brim.

"When?"

"Three weeks ago."

"Three weeks! But Papa's letter said…"

---

*An exclamation of surprise

"Lizzie," Sarah took her hand, "Papa … he wrote you five weeks ago. She hung on for you Liz, but you didn't come. So the next week I wrote also; to the people of that house, asking them please to find your address because our mother is dying and she so much wants to see you. We only had that Durban address. We didn't know where to find you." Sarah squeezed the words out through her sobs. Lizzie put her hand against the wall, she thought she was going to faint. Sarah grabbed hold of her.

"Come into the kitchen, I'll make some bush tea."

She sat Lizzie down on a kitchen chair.

"When did you get the letter?"

"Yesterday," Lizzie said, hearing her own voice as if coming from afar. Yesterday now felt like an eternity ago.

"Yesterday! Ag my sussie*, and you're here already!" No reproach now in Sarah's voice. "How did you get here?"

Lizzie explained her present position and Ben bringing her down.

"How is Papa?" She said when she had finished.

"Sober, thank the Lord, Hallelujah!"

Hallelujah, yes, still all the hallelujahs the family is hanging onto, Lizzie thought as thankfully, she felt herself stepping back into her old self, released from the pull of the emotional moment.

"Did he earn that much that he could buy you this house? Or did Samuel and Bennett pay money to it so that our Mama could at least *die* in a decent place."

Sarah seemed to not notice Lizzie's bitterness against the drunkard that she had to call Papa. She was preoccupied in weighing her words.

"Lizzie, I don't know how I can say this to you but…"

Lizzie's senses became alert and all feelings around her father's failures faded. Instinctively she knew that something big was coming at her. She straightened herself in her chair.

---

* Afrikaans for little sister as a term of endearment.

"What is it Sarah? Tell me!" The urgency in her voice seemed to force Sarah to blunder it out.

"You see, Joshua, he…"

"Joshua! For Christ sake, is he here? Does he live here?" she jumped up and clutched Sarah's arm.

"No! No, not any more."

"How do you mean not any more? Speak man, speak!"

Sarah's eyes were big and her face had paled. The grating sound of keys in the front door brought Lizzie to her senses.

"Sarah!" It was her father's croaky voice all right. "Where are you Sarah?"

"In the kitchen Papa. The good Lord has brought our Lizzie home."

"Lizzie? Lizzie!" There was a fast shuffle down the passage to the kitchen.

Lizzie turned around and looked at him: a grey old man, toothless, deeply carved wrinkles and watery blue eyes. There was no smell of drink on him. Sober as Sarah had said, sober and with a humble demeanour about him now.

"Papa!" Lizzie embraced him. "How are you Papa?"

He squinted as if he had difficulty seeing her, then he became tearful. "She's gone Lizzie, gone. The good Lord took her to a better place."

Lizzie felt herself tighten up and she withdrew from his embrace. She was a million miles away from these people – her family. But right now she *had* to know where Joshua was. She turned to Sarah. She was calm now.

"You were saying about Joshua."

"Ah, a good man he was," her father was muttering, fumbling with his waist coat buttons, "A good lad."

Lizzie exploded. "A good man! A good man! Jesus, Pa, he killed my baby!" She was beside herself; there was no shred of fear in her now. She knew that if Joshua walked through that door this minute she would spit at him, scratch his eyes out, slap his drunken face! "I could kill him!" She shouted as she flung her arms out, on the verge of hysteria.

"Ag, no need Lizzie, he already done that himself."

Lizzie's arms dropped to her side. She stood dead still. "What did you say? Is Joshua dead?"

"Hanged him self," his voice trembled. He looked down on the black and white linoleum, "come October four years ago," he whispered respectfully.

The relief was too much for Lizzie, her legs just gave way under her and she found herself sitting flat on the kitchen floor. Then the laughter came, uncontrollable, on and on. She wanted to shout *He can never beat me up again!* – but she couldn't speak for the hysterical laughter.

Sarah threw a mug of cold water in her face. Lizzie gasped and stopped. She sat there on the kitchen floor, shoulders bent with the water dripping from her. After a while she lifted her head and glared at her father.

"And so that makes him a good man; 'cause he removed his brutal carcass from this earth?"

Sarah came to sit on the floor too, facing Lizzie, taking her hand.

"This house: he left it to us in his will. Our Mama, she had a home of her own for a few years of her life, she didn't have to work no more."

A home of her own; her and her mother's dream, Lizzie thought as she wiped the water from her chin and looked at Sarah as her sister continued.

"He sold the one you lived in, said he couldn't bear to be there after what he'd done. He came to us plenty times after you left; all the way from Cape Town, always to beg our forgiveness, said one day he will make good for his sins. But Mama refused to give him your address and when you never answered her letters, she told him that we don't even know if you're still alive. He kept begging for forgiveness until one day Mama told him firmly: *Joshua, now you stop coming here. What difference will our forgiveness make to what has happened? It is God you must ask for forgiveness and after that you must forgive*

yourself so that you can live with yourself again. After
that we never heard no more of him until the solicitor's
letter came to tell us about this house and the money in the
bank. So you see Lizzie, this is your house, a home of
your own."

A home of my own, Lizzie thought that night when she lay
in bed, in a room of her own with her family who never
each had a room to themselves before Joshua's
inheritance. Sarah had explained to her the terms of the
will: the house was bequeathed to her and if she could not
or would not accept it, to her mother. They had written to
her but of course she was no longer in Durban and the
letter was returned. There were bitter thoughts in her:
Joshua lived in this house, perhaps even slept in this very
room! She shuddered, then calmed herself: he could never
enter it again; physically he could no longer harm her. She
thought of how Ben had made her aware of her fear that
she could kill him if she saw him again. Now she didn't
even have to concern herself about that; Joshua had done
that for her.

She thought about her mother and guilt lay heavily on
her heart. It occurred to her that the nightmare dream she
had when she had bronchitis, about her mother telling her
that she must forgive Joshua, was round about the time her
mother was dying and they were trying to find her. Is that
why her mother hung on, waiting for her? Is that what she
wanted to say to her? "Is that it Mama?" she asked the
empty room. A softness came over her as she thought of
her mother living in this nice three bed-roomed house, her
lifelong dream fulfilled. And the money that Joshua had
left to her specifically. She could see her mother resting
her rough, work worn, hands in her lap, sitting out in the
sun in the enclosed back yard and getting up after sunrise
in the mornings, not rushing out to clean and clean some
more. It was the only redeeming factor she could think of.
"Even so Mama," she said to the room, "forgiving Joshua
is a very tall order."

Then she thought that she herself, while being in this house, her house, had no need to get up early to pander to Mr. Mynhard's demands. When the thought struck her it came as quite a shock: she need not go back to work for him anymore. She could stay here in Cape Town. Find work, enrol in a college, get some qualifications under her belt, make a life for herself.

Miriam! That was the thunderbolt that hit her. She thought of that desperate night when she learned that they were going to take Miriam away from her and her fanciful plans to take her and run away to where they could not find them. Now she would have somewhere to take Miriam and give her a life amongst other children of her own age. But this thought was just as fanciful. The law would forbid it. Mr. Mynhard was now fostering her. He had, in the eyes of Social Services, the means to give her many advantages in life.

She heard some rowdy youths passing by in the street and she only now really noticed the heavily fortified windows: double bars, one on the inside and one on the outside, thick iron bars. In the Berg they have only a few flimsy bars on the bedroom windows and no gate across the front door. After fourteen years she had come back to a world that should be familiar - and yes Table Mountain was still there towering over the city; the bay as blue as ever; Lions head; Signal hill, and all the other well known landmarks, but something in the air, in the subtle feel of things, had changed. Or was it she who had changed?

Her mind flitted back to the Berg, and she remembered Mr. Mynhard's anxious eyes when she and Ben were leaving, and his voice: *"You will come back won't you Lizzie?"* He must have had a premonition of the possibilities she now had in her life. Oh, so many choices, so many emotions to deal with, and who could help her? Ben? Perhaps: it might be good to talk to him. But deep down she knew she would have to sort this out herself. She felt very tired and sleepy. Tomorrow in the light of day she could look at things again.

Miriam quickly saw that Maria was a fast learner and very willing, so she showed her how to do some of the things Aunty Lizzie had expected her to do thus she had more free time. She had also managed to wangle permission out of Mr. Bruno to skip her after lunch rest times if the weather was good, and the outdoors beckoned.

He had just nodded. "OK, as long as the house is kept quiet while I have my rest." She now had some time to herself to do with what *she* wanted to do, or simply to sit and be.

The meeting with Hester had changed things inside her. When she was catapulted into Mr. Bruno's straight-jacketed routine, and was so desperately unhappy trying to cope with it, she had often felt consoled by the marble hand, one of her friends – stroking it; and her eagle, painting it – looking at it, both in the sky and on the painting. But now that she knew why her mother had left her, she no longer saw herself as the foundling, the abandoned child. She felt that her mother's love lived inside her. This love made her strong.

When she sat out in the veld with the sun stroking her face, adoring the rugged mountain standing there so calm and undisturbed, her mind sometimes wandered to her old school and her playmates. It felt like a time so long ago that she could hardly remember herself as she was then. What would she say to them if she met them now? What did she say to them the few times she wrote letters to them? Letters they never answered. Perhaps their periods had also started, they might have breasts too. They could talk about *that*. Still, she felt as if she was years older than them and might not be able to talk to them in the same way they talked to each other.

It was during this time of her lonely wanderings that she became aware of something slowly happening to her. It was quite strange, and yet in some vague way, she felt it had always been with her. From time to time, she saw light in and around her body, especially in her hands. She discovered that she could play with it; if she bounced her hands gently off each other, she could clearly feel something moving between them, getting shorter and longer with each in and out movement, like an elastic band. Often just before she saw the light, she could feel a strong throbbing in the centre of her hands, almost like an engine vibrating, yet much, much more delicately; a very pleasant sensation. She loved it. At times she could see colours too; weaving themselves wave after wave in and through her body: pink, purple, gold, blue.

One day when she returned from the veld and saw Filamon tending the garden, she became aware of light around him. She watched him intently and could see it moving along with the movements of his body as he worked and sang, sometimes brighter, other times only faintly. She walked on.

Mr. Bruno was sitting on the veranda and the contrast of what was around the two of them was startling. Around Mr. Bruno she saw a dull, murky grey colour, but no light. She saw his lame hand resting on his lap like a lump of dead flesh. At the same time she felt the centres of her hands vibrating vigorously. She thought of the previous occasions, when, on impulse, she had massaged the hand, but then she did not have these feelings in her hands, and it was before she became aware of the light in and around her. She knew she had to take that hand in hers and do something with it: what, she did not know yet. The dogs came up to her and she realized that she could see the light around them too. Cinnamon had a lively, brilliant light, while Honey's was slow-moving, and dullish.

She took her hat off and sat down.

"How far did you go?" Mr. Bruno asked.

"Just to the flat stone."

"I don't like you going that far from the house without the dogs."

"But it wasn't the time for their walk Mr. Bruno, so I couldn't take them."

"Hmm, well perhaps they can have a walk more often, they might like that – at least, Cinnamon will."

"Mr. Bruno," she said cautiously, "please will you let me do some work on your hand?"

"What sort of work?" He sounded surprised.

"I don't really know right now... but let me just start and see what happens?"

He nodded and she picked up his hand and held it firmly between hers. She closed her eyes and became aware of violet light coming from what felt like a place between her eyebrows. It seemed to her that all she needed to do was to concentrate on it as it beamed itself on their three hands clasped together. They sat like that for the best part of twenty minutes before she felt the violet flame fading and the vibrations in her hands slowing. She knew it was time to let go of his hand. She gently laid it back on his lap.

Mr. Bruno turned his wheelchair around and headed indoors. At the French Doors he stopped, half turned and said, "Thank you," before he wheeled himself down the passage. It wasn't time for him to go to his room. Miriam smiled: she had been given a reprieve from her afternoon 'imprisonment', the dogs were now allowed to walk whenever she walked, and Mr. Bruno was apparently going to have an unscheduled rest. The rigid rules too were becoming like an elastic band. She felt elated, but knew it had little to do with the relaxed rules, or any other circumstance in her life. The joy was coming from inside her. She took a last look at the setting sun kissing the mountain, and then went inside to help Maria prepare supper.

Bruno closed his bedroom door behind him and sat there in his wheelchair, crying. He did not know why he was crying, but he just let the tears roll down like a baby would. After a while he lifted himself onto his bed and fell fast asleep, a deep dreamless sleep.

He woke up from the clatter of crockery and cutlery. He was not annoyed, he felt calm inside himself, like a still lake. He got up and wheeled himself into the dining area. Maria was just leaving and Miriam was putting the finishing touches to the meal. She stirred the Marie Rose sauce a final time before pouring it over the fish dish, then tested the sprouts: not too soft, not too hard, just as she was taught to cook it to maintain most of its nutritional value. The other vegetables underwent the same scrutiny.

They ate in silence for a while, then Bruno said:

"Will you do that again sometime?" He pointed to the lame hand.

Miriam beamed. "Gladly Mr. Bruno, gladly," and after a while, "We can set time aside every afternoon for the work, if you like?" Bruno nodded.

The telephone rang and Bruno frowned. "Who could that be ringing at our supper time?"

Miriam got up. "It's past our usual supper time Mr. Bruno, you had a long rest." She picked the receiver up and then a wide smile shot across her face. "Aunty Lizzie!"

Bruno put his knife and fork down. A strange foreboding had taken hold of him. He steered his wheelchair across to the 'phone and took it from Miriam. She was hovering close to it, trying to catch what Lizzie was saying so he put it on speakerphone. They listened in amazement to her account of her changed circumstances, Bruno hardly saying a word. She finished by saying: "So Mr. Mynhard it will be a couple of weeks or more before I'll be back, there's quite a few things here that need to be looked at."

Bruno's heart dropped into his stomach as he croaked: "As long as you do come back Lizzie; we need you here!"

"Of course Mr. Mynhard! May I have a few words with Miriam please?"

Bruno switched the speakerphone off: he would let them have their privacy, but he watched Miriam's facial expressions hoping it would give him the desperately longed for reassurance. But he could find nothing in it.

Back at the table he pushed his plate away and sat staring out in front of him. Miriam too had lost her appetite. She cleared the table.

They went to their rooms early that night. Bruno lay awake for a long time with questions and thoughts flitting through his mind: *What if Lizzie leaves me? But would she? That would mean leaving Miriam too. Yes, but what will happen when Miriam turns sixteen and is allowed to make her own choices? How will the state of my health be by then?* He hadn't thought that far in the future before, and it made him shiver. He realized that he had assumed that Miriam would stay with him always – that he would provide for her: education, material comforts, in short all her needs. He hadn't thought realistically about her future. The hands on his clock showed half-past one before he eventually drifted into sleep.

The dream was vivid and frightening: he was at his father's grave. At the top end, where his mother had erected an angel with hands spread out in blessing, was a very tall man standing dressed in a black hat and cloak. He looked at Bruno, pointing to the grave.

"Exhume him!" he commanded.

Bruno put his face in his hands, "I can't, it's too awful!"

"Exhume him!" the figure shouted. "Exhume him or you will go into that grave with him!"

Bruno woke from the shaking of his bed. His lame hand, which he had put on his chest before he had dozed off, was lying on the bed next to him, yet he was still lying on his back, his whole body shaking, shaking the bed underneath him. He felt like a helpless child, terrified, and put the light on. It was ten to six. A shimmer of light was creeping through the curtains, and the thought that Filamon would soon be around and that Miriam would open the door to let the dogs out, comforted him somewhat. He went to pick up his hand but stopped in mid air: the middle finger twitched, ever so slightly, and then stopped. Bruno let out a long sigh and brought the lame hand to rest on his heart, stroking it gently as he watched the light through the curtains growing brighter.

Miriam overslept the morning after Aunty Lizzie's phone call and was awoken by Maria's constant knocking at the back door and Mr. Bruno calling her. The dogs were scratching and whining at the French Windows, desperate to get out.

Though she had gone to her room the same time as Mr. Bruno did, she had not gone to sleep. She had fumbled underneath her bed, and pulled out a thick physiology book, which she 'pinched' from Mr. Bruno's large collection while he was having his unusual sleep. She was curious about the muscles, ligaments, sinews and nerves and the workings of the human hand. The thought came to her that she might be able to visualize them when she next did the work. It was way past her usual bedtime before she had put out her light and fallen into a deep sleep.

She got up, let the dogs out first, and then opened the back door for Maria before she went to Mr. Bruno's room expecting a scolding. He was still in bed and the first thing she noticed was the lame hand resting on his heart and his left hand stroking it.

"Miriam," he said, "the middle finger twitched a few times this morning."

There was no telling her off, only awe in his voice. She walked round the bed to take a closer look at the hand. The colour was slightly less grey but there was still no light in it. Nevertheless Miriam was excited.

"We'll work on it again today. I'm sorry I overslept this morning Mr. Bruno."

She saw a deep smile spreading across his face as he nodded.

"We will work after you'd taken the dogs for their walk later in the afternoon," he said as she left the room.

Miriam was enjoying the new freedom she had, and that helped her not to miss Aunty Lizzie so much. She, Miriam, was the mistress of the house for now. Mr. Bruno was now wholly dependent on her, and that made him more lenient so that she could sneak in little requests that he would previously not have granted.

Then there was this experimenting with his hand. She wondered if he would have allowed it if Aunty Lizzie was here? Maybe he was agreeing to it only because he was so desperate. Yes, he did allow her to massage it before she had become aware of the light, but it was at that time when he was angry because of the attention Ben and Aunty Lizzie were giving each other. What would Aunty Lizzie, have said about it? Would she have approved? So long as Aunty Lizzie was away she could freely enjoy this new thing that was coming into her, and maybe help Mr. Bruno with it. It was all very exciting and as long as she was sure that Aunty Lizzie would come back she didn't mind if she stayed away for quite a few weeks… and yet, Ben: they were together in Cape Town. That was a worrying thought. She often took the painting of him out, and longed to show it to him and hear his praise, hear what he thought about the frightened little boy's look in his eyes. She could talk to Ben; really talk to him - open her heart. She loved Ben and she loved Aunty Lizzie – oh what a difficult thing this was! Yet sometimes when she played with the light in her hands, and with her breath drew it deep inside her until it flooded her body and beyond, nothing seemed difficult. It didn't matter that Ben and Aunty Lizzie seemed to love each other and that she would rather that he loved only her. At those times love was love, big enough to hold everyone in its embrace, and she felt those two words of the voice, *Possessiveness and jealousy,* just melting away. But the moments when that bliss engulfed her like a wave were rare, and more often she felt jealous of Aunty Lizzie, the one woman on earth that she really loved. It was all so very complicated and much easier to look at the physiology of the hand, and to see if this light that just came to her might be used to heal.

So she put her mind to the work she wanted to do with Mr. Bruno, feeling very grateful that he allowed her to do it and seemed to be enthusiastic about it too.

A week had gone by with Miriam working on Bruno's hand every afternoon yet there was no further movement in it. Bruno felt very down that night when he went to bed, wondering if the whole affair was just the imaginings of a girl in her puberty. He covered himself up carefully with an extra blanket; autumn was beginning to show signs of approaching, and the weather in the Berg could change quite suddenly, especially at night.

He fell asleep almost straight away. He was walking across a field on a cold dark night. A thin layer of cloud that stretched across the wide expanse of sky had wiped out the stars, and swallowed the half moon that had been there the night before. Yet Bruno could see everything clearly as if he was an owl whose vision was enhanced by the darkness: the grass swaying slightly in the gentle breeze, the trees dropping dead leaves here and there adding to the brown and gold pile on the ground, a cricket calling its mate. It was all very peaceful.

Unexpectedly, the graveyard loomed up in front of him, and there was the black clad man again. His heart started thumping in his chest and he tried to turn, but his legs were carrying him away from where he wanted to go: anywhere, except to where they were going, straight to his father's grave and the menacing figure.

Then he saw it… oh how awful! The marble slab was slowly lifting as the stone angel stood watching. He was unable to move, totally paralysed. With the slab removed, the soil just seemed to clear itself from the coffin. Then the lid creaked as inch-by-inch, it opened. Bruno wanted at least to look away, but again there was no mercy. His head was held in a clamp and his eyes were fixed on it, he could not even close them. The creaking stopped and the coffin lay open. He stared:

It was completely empty.

Or was it? ... No, not quite. He squinted and then he made sense of its contents: two lame legs lying there, shrivelled up. And they started to talk to him, no, begging him: "Take us out of here please, take us out of here, we want to walk!"

Anger rose from the pit of his stomach like a huge uncontrollable wave almost choking him.

"But it's *his* coffin!" he croaked, and then he got his voice back: "Don't you see? It has nothing to do with me, it's *him* who put you in there, the brute!"

The dark figure moved closer to him and he felt the chill of the night penetrating his bones.

"Take another look. Do you see him in there?"

"No!"

"Were his legs lame?"

"No, but…"

"Whose legs are they?"

Bruno was silent, trying to cast his fixed stare towards the overcast sky, but they would not move.

The voice became fierce. "Whose legs are they!"

Bruno's shoulders started shaking.

"Mine, mine," he sobbed, "mine!"

"Love us, love us!" the legs had started pleading again and the desperation in their voices reverberated through the quiet night.

The man took his black hat off and held it to his heart in a gesture of the deepest respect.

"All our sins are forgiven," he said, and his voice echoed through the still air, "All our sins are forgiven," and then he disappeared into the night.

The echo was still in Bruno's ears when he woke up... 'All our sins are forgiven'.

He lay very still, holding on to the feeling of peace inside him. It was pitch black in the room, yet it felt to him that there was no darkness anywhere because his body was illuminating everything. He had no need for thoughts, he was resting in a sense of immeasurable security: there was nothing to worry about, nothing he had to control. He drifted into a deep dreamless sleep.

The Sunday morning tranquillity filled the valley. The sky was a clear blue and the mountain stood proud in all its glory allowing the sun to stroke its peaks, painting it into a pink glow. Cinnamon sat statue-still on the edge of the garden where it sloped down towards the Protea bushes in the veld below. Honey was lying next to her, head resting on her paws, eyes moving this way and that way, scanning the scenery from her relaxed pose.

Miriam was getting the breakfast ready; it was Maria's day off. She heard the squeak of Mr. Bruno's wheelchair coming down the passage and took the steaming bowls of porridge to the table.

"Miriam," he said, "pull a chair out for me and put a cushion on it."

He had his walking stick with him and stopped the wheelchair a yard or so from the table. She saw him slowly but determinedly get out of it, and holding his stick tightly in his good hand, he shuffled to the chair she had prepared for him. She stood watching him manoeuvring himself onto the chair holding her breath. When he was finally comfortably seated, she let out a deep sigh and felt a surge of joy going through her body. There was Mr. Bruno sitting in front of her, not dull skinned, dark, brooding, but with pride in his eyes. He looked so pleased with himself.

All through their silent meal she watched him whenever she thought he wasn't noticing. There was a change in him that she couldn't put a finger on, but what was certain was that there was a lightness to his body, an aliveness. She couldn't see the sort of light around his body that she could see around Filamon, but it was good to look at him. She looked for his hand, but it was lying on his lap, not displayed on the table.

"Any more movement in the hand Mr. Bruno?" she asked, subtly coaching him to put it in sight.

"Not yet," he said, smiling at her brightly.

Miriam felt cheered up, and then she saw it: the faintest, just the faintest light around his body. Her joy spread across her face, and they sat there looking at each other like two conspirators.

When breakfast was over, Miriam wanted to push his wheelchair closer to him, but he held his hand up: "No, leave it." With the aid of his stick he shuffled to the chair, eased himself into it, and steered it out to the veranda.

Miriam cleared the table and got on with the housework, but every now and then she looked at him through the French doors. She saw that he had his lame hand on his lap and was massaging it gently all the time.

The sun had left the mountain peaks and was spotlighting the humble houses deep down in the valley. Bruno's eyes followed the shifting light and he thought of the empty coffin: his dad had gone, disappeared totally, no skeleton, nothing, just his own legs, pleading for love and a chance to walk. He had lost all desire to analyse or make sense of the dream. It didn't matter anymore: his dad's anger and violence; *It's all gone; over, forgotten.*

Dispassionately he thought about his own anger. But when it came to his violence towards Valerie his mouth twitched slightly with shame, and the guilt surfacing threatened to unsettle his peacefulness. Automatically his mind reached for the coffin, the coffin where he had buried so many unwanted feelings, dangerous feelings. Suddenly a light was switched on in his mind, and he understood: the two shrivelled up legs! All incorporated in them!

"My God!" he said, banging his hand on his forehead.

He sat like that, eyes closed, for a long time, and when he opened them he saw the lame hand, the hand that had sent Valerie flying down the stairs and put the fear into Ben's eyes, the fear that he saw in Miriam's picture of him.

"Oh my God", he said again, "what have I done to myself?"

CHAPTER 8

Lizzie had a long lie-in the morning after her arrival. She was tired. It was a long drive from the Berg, all through the night and most of Easter Monday. Inside she felt like a jigsaw puzzle scattered about. It would be an enormous task to put all the pieces together so that she could make sense of the picture life was now holding up to her. Hunger got her out of bed. In the kitchen she saw one place laid for breakfast with a note next to it.

Tuesdays I work only till half past two. Mealiepap on the stove. Eggs in the fridge for omelettes for lunch. Papa won't be back from work till this evening. See you later. Sarah.

Lizzie sat down to a heaped up plate of thick yellow mealy porridge, which had been slowly plopping away on the stove-plate. She ate with relish. This is what Mama used to cook for us, she thought. When she had finished, she washed up, tidied around and went into the bathroom. There was a shower over the bath and she soaked herself under it for a long time, allowing her thoughts to roam around. She was longing for her mother, thinking of her living in this nice house. A sense of deep gratitude for the few years of grace she had been given seeped in and around her heart, yet it made her feel slightly uncomfortable. She did not want to give Joshua credit for it. If she believed in the Hallelujah God of her family she could have prostrated herself before the statue of the Virgin Mary and cried out her thanks, punctuated by many Hallelujahs. But she didn't. She now felt only embarrassment at the thought of it.

She got out of the shower and rubbed herself dry vigorously until her skin tingled, then dressed and went out into the back garden. The first thing she noticed was the iron-gate with its large padlock refusing entry to the enclosed space. The autumn sun was bright, with still enough warmth in it to entice her to sit on the padded bench and let her limbs go limp in total surrender to relaxation. How nice it was to just sit and do nothing, not thinking of a time schedule, she thought.

She must have fallen asleep because the opening of the kitchen door startled her. Sarah came out.

"You had no lunch my Lizzie!"

Lizzie smiled and patted the seat next to her.

"Come and sit down. The sun made me fall asleep."

They sat together, chatting away. Sarah told Lizzie about her job at the supermarket, and ended with "The pay is good and we get the foodstuff cheap. The out of date stuff we can take for free. And Papa, he has a soft job, looking after the cars in the car park. So we eat well."

After a while Lizzie said: "Sarah, I want to go and see our Mama's grave. Where is she buried?"

Lizzie felt a caution coming in the air between them, and a sense of foreboding took hold of her.

"We'll take you there, we go every Sunday," she said. "But …Lizzie," Sarah took a deep breath and spat the words out quickly: "We buried her next to Joshua."

The blood drained from Lizzie's head. She was near fainting.

"You buried our Mama next to a murderer!!"

Sarah put her head into her hands and started crying.

"You can't understand Lizzie," she said through her sobs. "Long time you know nothing about hunger and cold any more. Mama coughing and coughing in the damp rooms on the wastelands of George; the potatoes, we hardly skinned them, trying to make them more to feed everybody. That was all we had, sometimes for months. The time when you sent that money from Durban – ai, we ate well my sussie, we ate well; and we bought a new blanket."

Lizzie clenched her hands together as though to contain the guilt from overwhelming her, knuckles showing white.

"When the good Lord gave us all this… well, He had opened His heaven to us. We talked and talked about it for days. Then the news came, about… how he died, and that it wasn't illness, and our Mama said: *If I didn't tell him not to come here anymore, he would not have done it. The Lord will punish me for that.*' But the Lord gave her time in a decent house and enough food to feed her family. When Samuel went into the army, he could give a permanent address to them; hold his head high." She was silent for a moment.

"When we came here, we went to his grave to say thank you to him and to say sorry we sent him away. We put a tombstone with some of the money he had left to Mama, and every Sunday we put flowers on his grave. One day Mama said: *Joshua wants more than flowers, he wants us to forgive him, that's what he wants.* So Mama went to the council and she booked and paid for the plot next to his grave. We went, the all five of us, and we stood around his grave, and we, each one of us told him we have forgiven him. Then Mama said: *Joshua, I will pray that one day Lizzie will forgive you too, and when my time comes, I will lie here next to you so that the memory of what you gave to us will always live in my children's hearts.*"

Lizzie felt the heat rising up in her chest, into her face and her head started itching as if head lice had invaded her thick black hair. She got up. There was harshness in her voice:

"I'd like to go by myself to Mama's grave. You just give me the address and directions."

The sun had lost its warmth and it was getting chilly in the back yard. They went inside to prepare the supper.

There was a hard painful knot sitting in Lizzie's stomach as she shredded the cabbage. The smell of fried onions and tomatoes filled the kitchen and conjured up the picture of her mother peeling potatoes, taking great pains to do it as thinly as possible. *And all those years of their hunger I could have sent them money.* Inside her the knot now felt huge. She knew how hard it was to feed five mouths. But she sent them a big sum of money once to placate her conscience, and then washed them off her, together with Joshua. All she wanted was to forget her pain, pretend it didn't exist, and they were thrown into oblivion too. Yet there was no reproach from them, they just welcomed her back into their bosom. Lizzie's thoughts stalled, like a horse in front of a ditch that was too wide to get over. The truth flooded in, unstoppable: *We are planets apart, my family and I.* She thought of her father, a toothless old man with whom she had very little contact as a child, and her siblings, so much younger than herself, crying at night in their cramped accommodation. Sarah was only six or seven when she left for Cape Town. And they were still singing Hallelujah to a God she did not believe in. She was struggling to understand something inside herself that was so subtle that her mind couldn't find words for it: some kind of Presence, coming to her on the rarest of occasions. That was the nearest she could get to God, if that was what one wanted to call it. How could she even begin to explain this to her family? Suddenly she felt desperately lonely. Standing alone against a barrage of sob stories, expecting her to forgive at the drop of a hat.

She heard her father come in and cringed. How did her mother live with him all those years? *Why* did she? Well, why did she herself stay with Joshua when he started hitting her? At least her father wasn't violent, didn't hit her mother – he just didn't provide for them. Perhaps she loved him. Did she love Joshua? She certainly was attracted to him, and him to her. But was that love? How do you know what love is when you're nineteen?

Ben came into her mind, and she toyed with the idea of taking up his offer to contact him if she needed him. She did not feel she could invite him here to her family, and she did not want to go to his home. It would have to be a neutral place.

Miriam persisted with the work on Mr. Bruno's hand, day after day. Things were changing, not so much in the hand, but rather in what was happening with the light. A couple of days previously the violet light had made way for a sparkling silvery light, bright and vibrant. It seemed as if it was coming in tiny rays, each one separately penetrating the muscles, ligaments and sinews that Miriam had clearly in her mind's eye. All she had to do was to concentrate on it. She was fascinated by this wonderful experience, which lasted for a couple of days.

Then something happened that scared her. When the sparkling light left, a thick black darkness surrounded the hand, something she had not seen before. It was almost as if she could smell putrid flesh. She let go of it as if it was a nest of worms. She noticed that Mr. Bruno had dozed off, so she just sat there watching the hand.

Then she saw it: there was movement in the black darkness. Slowly, very slowly it was lifting itself from the hand and it seemed to her it was beginning to move to the left of it. She looked in that direction and sat transfixed: a large edgeless ball of brilliant white light had formed a kind of a funnel between itself and the hand. It looked to Miriam as if it was drawing the darkness out of the limb. This went on for several minutes before it stopped. At the same time Mr. Bruno woke up, so Miriam got up. She felt quite overwhelmed by the experience and wanted to be by herself. She announced the end of the session and Mr. Bruno said: "Thank you Miriam", but remained seated where he was.

She went into her room and shut the door. She was frightened. *What am I letting myself in for? The light was one thing, but that horrible darkness!* She could still see it as if it was hovering right in front of her.

The voice came unexpectedly. *Don't give the darkness power by focussing on it. Focus on the light!*

She sat, startled. She hadn't heard the voice for a long time now, and certainly not as clearly as this. Automatically she took a deep breath, and then another. She felt calmer, and the thoughts in her head were almost as if she was speaking to herself: *Let go of the fear Miriam, you are safe in the light.* She knew these were her own thoughts and not the voice speaking to her. There were more thoughts in her mind and it occurred to her that this horrid experience could in fact have been a good thing. If that silvery light had loosened the diseased energies in the hand, then the debris needed to be cleared away, didn't it? So maybe another kind of light was needed for that, sucking it up like a vacuum cleaner. She felt excited by this idea. "Could be, could be," she kept saying to herself out loud. Who could tell her if she was right? For a brief moment she thought of asking Mr. Bruno if she could look on the Net for an answer, but it didn't feel right. It seemed that anything from the outside would be like an intrusion into an experience so very private and sacred to her. Trust; she felt she just needed to trust that which came from within her. She reached for her hat; a walk in the late afternoon sunshine would clear her head.

On Lizzie's first Sunday at home she made excuses when Sarah and her father made their weekly pilgrimage to her mother's grave – and that of Joshua: headache, period pains. True, but excuses nevertheless.

The following week she made an appointment to see the solicitor with whom Joshua's will was lodged. Her appointment was for 3.30. She decided to go in early and explore Cape Town and the changes that had taken place since she last lived there, working for Mrs. de Waal in the suburb of Constantia.

She took a train into Cape Town and a bus from the city centre to the Waterfront. The hours slipped away as she marvelled at the handcrafted gifts in the Waterfront Craft market and other shops. People were bustling around, and she felt exhilarated by all the life going on around her – noisy, colourful, voices competing in extolling the beauty and usefulness of their wares. The delicious smell of spices hung around and mingled with the salty sea air she was breathing in, tasting it on her tongue.

She treated herself to lunch in the Quay Four Restaurant and sat transfixed by the superb view of the harbour, the coming and going of boats. She was lucky; there was a free concert by the Cape Town Philharmonic Orchestra that day in the large Agfa Amphitheatre. Lizzie lost herself in the music. There were no thoughts of Joshua and her family, no guilt.

At three o'clock she made her way back to the city centre. Her stomach tightened as she entered the building where the solicitor dealing with the case had his office. Joshua was looming large within her.

The receptionist showed her in – "Mr. Phillips, Mrs Aronson." They shook hands and he gestured to a comfortable leather clad chair. She sat, feeling small and insignificant, not like a woman who was coming to sign documents to accept her property. Her property... it was still a very strange feeling: she owned a house, all paid for. Her hands shook slightly as she signed the precious papers.

When she had finished and put the pen down, Mr. Phillips looked at her from behind his black-rimmed glasses, pushing them nervously up on his nose. He cleared his throat and got up.

"There is something else Mrs. Aronson." .

From a small cabinet behind him he took out a bunch of keys, unlocked a drawer in his desk, and produced a letter.

"My client gave strict instructions that this was to be given to you personally, and to you alone. If for some reason this was no longer possible, it was to be destroyed." He put the letter in front of her on the desk.

Outside the seagulls were squabbling over the crumbs on the windowsill, battling against the sudden wind that threatened to knock them off course, but Lizzie was oblivious to it. All she could see was that familiar handwriting, those beautifully formed letters slanting symmetrically across the envelope. Joshua's handwriting was unique. She would recognize it amongst a million others. The love letters he wrote to her during their courtship – when she sorted out the mail in Mrs. de Waal's house – would catch her eye, she hardly needed to look to see who it was addressed to, and she remembered the flutter in her heart: oh the joy!

But this was no love letter – Joshua was dead, Joshua who had killed her baby. She looked at the letter as if it was a serpent that could strike at any moment.

As from afar she heard Mr. Phillips' voice, and saw the form he had put in front of her, next to the letter, that envelope with the beautiful handwriting on it.

"If you could just sign acceptance please."

Automatically she signed. She was amazed that there was no shaking of her hand now. A deadly calm had come over her as she put 'Joshua' in her handbag. She got up, shook hands with Mr. Phillips and left the building.

Outside in the sun, she stood still for a moment, then took the letter out and dangled it between her thumb and fore-finger, *I can do with you what I want now Joshua! I can put you in the fire, unread; I can throw you in the gutter; I can feed you to the fish in the pond over there, and you can do nothing about it – nothing!'* She looked at it for a while longer, then put it back in her handbag and walked to the train station.

By the time she had boarded the train the strange, almost sinister, calm had left her. Guilt about her mother had crept back into her mind, multiplying with every mile that sped by. She felt terrible. She needed someone to talk to. She decided to talk things over with Ben.

When she got home she phoned him. He sounded pleased to hear from her.

"Ben," she said, "there's something I'd like to talk to you about. Could we meet?"

"Sure, I've got an easy morning on Friday, we could meet for tea. How about the open air Café in the Gardens at eleven o'clock? Could you make that?"

Lizzie was very glad to be away from home again, especially as Sunday was approaching and she dreaded the anticipated disapproval on her father and Sarah's faces if she refused again to go with them to the cemetery, especially as she hadn't been by herself either.

She left early so that she could explore more old familiar places by herself before her meeting with Ben. She felt happier within herself as she watched, from the train window, Table Mountain coming closer and closer. She could see the play of light and colours as the sun shifted its angle, highlighting a rock-cluster now, then another one later.

From the train station she walked up Adderley Street and passed St. George's Cathedral with its beautiful stained glass windows. She turned into the National Library, browsing, drinking in the tranquillity, the silence, and above all the smell of books, the old valuable volumes housed there.

When she left the library she still had time before their meeting, so she ambled down tree-lined Government Avenue. She had always loved the cool shade that the tall old oak trees provided, and she stopped every few yards or so to look up at the branches dancing in the breeze. A squirrel darted down a tree trunk and scampered in and out of a clump of autumn leaves. She stopped and watched his movements for a while; then looked at her watch - it was nearly eleven and she quickened her pace.

The Café came into view and she saw Ben was waiting. She thought that there was a concerned look on his face; almost as he was expecting her to be in trouble. He helped her take off her light coat and pulled a chair out for her, then went to sit opposite her, waiting.

"Ben," she said, "Joshua is dead." He looked shocked. "Don't worry, I didn't kill him. He hung himself almost four years ago."

Then a puzzling thing happened. She saw gladness spontaneously spring up into his eyes, making them sparkle.

"So you're no longer married!"

She sat stunned.

"No, no I guess not."

For her the relief was purely about the fact that he could no longer beat her up, nor was there any more danger that she could attack him. But Ben's eyes... she was puzzled by the keenness in them when he said that. Intuitively she knew that now was not the time to talk to him about the letter that was burning in her handbag, had been burning there ever since she put it there.

They ordered tea and scones and she filled him in on the details, finally ending with: "So many opportunities, so many decisions to make now, and yet..."

"And that's what you wanted to talk to me about? That 'and yet'?"

She nodded. "How can I leave her alone in that lonely place for another four or more years? She is my child, the only one I have."

"At the moment," Ben replied.

Lizzie stared at him.

"You mean..."

"You're a young woman yet Lizzie, you could have more children of your own you know. You're a free woman now. You could do many things with your life here in town: further your education, getting a good job, having a social life."

Ben had leaned forward oozing enthusiasm, but he stopped abruptly.

"Sorry Lizzie, I got carried away". He straightened himself up and assumed a formal posture almost as if he was with a client. "That's not what the real issue is, is it? Joshua, dead or alive still lives in you, directing your life."

Lizzie shuddered, tugging at her handbag.

"You haven't even thought of yourself as a woman who could get married and have children. To you all men are just Joshua, and the only child in your life to love, is Miriam."

"But I brought her up!"

Lizzie saw the frustration in Ben's eyes as she veered away from the frightening issue of men and became uncomfortable when he made no reply, just sat there, body slumped, lips pursed. They ate their scones in silence. Only the birds were holding a jolly conversation in the swinging branches above them.

"Lizzie," Ben said when he picked up the bill, "you will have to sort out this thing in you, yourself. Retreating to the 'safe haven' of The Berg is always an option, of course. It is a question of choices."

Lizzie felt as if something hard inside her was cracking, breaking up, crumbling, and she wanted to get away from Ben whom she saw as the cause of all this discomfort. They hugged briefly when they parted and she watched him walking away: back stiff, shoulders climbing towards his ears. She felt dreadful - and she didn't want to go home where guilt surfaced every time she became aware of her own selfishness all those years when her family was suffering, her mother struggling and longing for her.

A cluster of pigeons pecked away at some seeds and crumbs. All of a sudden their peace was shattered as cannon fire boomed across the city from Signal Hill, announcing the noon hour. Bewildered they flew up in the air, wings flapping, squawking in dismay.

Lizzie took a deep breath. *What shall I do with my shattered peace?* She asked herself. A sugarbird flew past, its long beak poised for an encounter with a Protea bush. She thought of the Protea garden in Kirstenbosch and decided to spend the afternoon walking in, and exploring, the Botanical Garden. She had always found it a very peaceful, often healing experience to be amongst so many beautiful plants, and her legs yearned to walk the stretch of forest on its outskirts. Perhaps nature, so close to the Mountain, would guide her in her decision-making.

Bruno felt a great change was taking place within him. Since the day after the coffin dream there were new

147

insights almost daily. Memories of his father kept popping up, ancient, long forgotten, presenting themselves in a bizarre kind of way: watching his father, bare backed, digging a vegetable patch over in the back garden, suddenly straightening up, slowly rubbing his thigh, his mouth a grimace of pain. How old was he then? Fifteen perhaps? But now, what most stood out in his memory was the long swollen mark across his back, as if the skin could only heal - sort of - by thickening itself like a bastion against pain. Pointing to the mark, he had asked:

"Is that a war wound?"

There was a flicker in his father's eyes, a kind of a shudder, and for a moment he thought he saw tears, but when his father blinked there were none.

His father shook his head, his lips pursed into a thin line. "War wounds one could cope with, they come from strangers," was all he said before he continued with the digging.

Now, seeing that scene playing itself off in his mind, he felt a deep compassion for his father and the traumas he suffered as a boy, and a man, and his self-defeating ways of dealing with them. Strange how vivid that memory was. He could even remember that the sun, at that moment, dipped behind the horizon, leaving bruised clouds in the sky, flaming at the edges.

But deep inside him, at the very edge of his awareness, he was grappling with a memory – the memory of two shrivelled up legs in the coffin, begging for love. He started stroking his hand again. Whenever he sat quietly by himself he would just spontaneously do this. He had also incorporated in his daily routine three short periods of taking a few steps, holding on to his walking stick, from his wheelchair to the table, and from the table to the wheelchair, and everyday he got out of the chair a little bit further from the table. Every time he felt elated when he had achieved his goal. And Miriam was there, applauding him with her smile and the joyful sparkle in her eyes.

It was on the Sunday morning when the Mountain foliage was beginning to display autumn colours, promising a feast for the eye in May, that Bruno discovered that he could move his fingers. At first he thought that he was having one of his vivid dreams again, but he kept on moving them and found that they were loose, moving effortlessly. The hand could not pick itself up, though it seemed to Bruno that it was less of a dead weight.

He called out to Miriam who was doing the dishes, and the urgency in his voice made her run out onto the veranda.

"What's the matter Mr. Bruno?"

"Look!" he pointed to his fingers and let them dance on his hand. "Look!"

Miriam stared. She started to rush towards him, but stopped in her tracks. Straightening herself, she put her hands on her heart, a gesture which reminded Bruno of the black clad man of the coffin dream when he said: 'All our sins are forgiven', and unexpectedly, to his great embarrassment, he burst into tears, unable to control himself. When his sobs subsided, he looked sheepishly at Miriam and saw the tears rolling down her cheeks. She was making no effort to stop them. They looked at each other and then, through her tears, Miriam smiled, one of her smiles that compelled the recipient to return it. Then she said, "I must get those dishes done Mr. Bruno" and disappeared into the house.

After lunch Bruno decided to phone Ben. He took the phone into his room.

"Ben", he said when they had exchanged the preliminaries, "first of all I want to say to you that you were right when you said that I had a lot of suppressed anger in me."

"Dad!" Bens voice sounded like he had never heard it before; was it pure surprise, or was there compassion in it too?

"I've been having quite a bit of insight into this family pattern you've been pointing out to me: again, you were quite right."

"Oh Dad – I don't know what to say!"

"Well then, let me tell you about an amazing thing. As I'm sitting here talking to you I can move the fingers of my right hand freely."

"What are you saying Dad?"

"I can't pick the hand up yet, but somehow it feels lighter than before."

"Good God! When did all this happen? What do you think has brought it about?"

Bruno told him about the work Miriam had been doing on his hand and their regular sessions.

"She doesn't want to say much about what she's doing, but she did say that she sees light, different kinds of light at different times penetrating the hand. Apparently she had secretly been studying the structure of hands from information in one of my old physiology books, and now as she holds my hand she keeps this knowledge in her mind and just let the light heal that area. This is something that has developed in her only recently, and I don't think she's quite sure what it is all about. It must be good because she is blooming and I am *so* much better.

"You sound it Dad."

"How is Lizzie?"

"I've only seen her once briefly; I think she is going through a bit of a rough time. Listen Dad, I'd like to come and see you – perhaps when Lizzie is ready to go back I can bring her up?"

"Thank you Ben, that would be really good."

After the call Bruno sat thinking. How long ago was it that he resented and feared Ben's attention to Lizzie? Scarcely four weeks, yet it felt like an eternity. That was when he realized that much more had changed than getting the life back in his fingers and the gradually developing strength in his legs. Inside him, it felt like a vast sea upon which he had set sail in a rickety boat. He felt small and vulnerable; yet somehow, deep within himself, he felt sure that he was heading towards the safety of a large ocean liner.

He stretched himself out on his bed and drifted into sleep.

Ten days had elapsed since Lizzie's visit to Kirstenbosch. Nothing spectacular happened on that walk, no revelation, no sudden insight, and no solution was given to her on a plate. Yet she had enjoyed the walk and felt refreshed when she headed back to the Cape Flats. Even so she was still putting off going to her mother's grave because Joshua would be there too, adorned by her family's weekly flowers. Inside her bag, his letter was still gnawing at her. On several occasions she had decided she would destroy it. Once she had actually struck a match when she was alone in the house and had held the letter up to it. For some reason the match went out. As she reached for another, she felt an enormous exhaustion washing over her and she abandoned the whole thing. It felt like some unseen hand had stopped her.

When at last she had got herself together enough to go to the grave, she chose a Monday when she hoped it would be quiet. She had bought flowers beforehand and walked in with a firm tread. *I am going to visit my mother's grave* she said to herself, *and Joshua can be there all he likes: I will not even look at him, just as I will not read his letter.*

This graveyard was new to her. There were huge oak trees on the edges and they seemed to her like sentinels, guarding the dead. Up in the sky dark clouds were terracing themselves against streaks of light. The smell of decaying leaves was all around her. She looked at the piece of paper in her hand – number 1065. Row on row the gravestones stood, like testimonies to transience.

She found her mother's yet unmade mound of ground easily and avoided looking at the ostentatious gravestone next to it. The flowers her family had placed on both graves quivered in the light breeze. The graveyard was, as she had anticipated, empty, except for an old woman sweeping up the leaves between the graves and clearing the ones on top of gravestones. A southeasterly wind had been blowing the night before. There were leaves on her mother's grave too and she knelt down to clear them before she arranged the flowers in a vase.

The old woman was coming closer, her broom leaving little piles of leaves in the pathways. Lizzie nodded a greeting and asked:

"Where can I get water?"

"The tap's over there." She pointed to it and Lizzie went to fill the vase.

When she came back the woman had swept up the leaves between Joshua and her mother's graves and she was moving further away. Lizzie placed her bunch of peace lilies firmly on her mother's grave and wondered what she should say to her, what words she could find to ask for forgiveness. Nothing stirred within her. It was like a flat, dead landscape. She waited some more but all that came was that dreadful tiredness washing over her again. She had to sit down but there was nowhere to sit – except on Joshua's gravestone. She cringed at the thought. The feeling that she was about to faint forced her hand so she sat down on the very edge of it.

"Mama," she half sobbed, "Mama, please! Can't you forgive me? I know I was so very selfish, I know, but Mama, please understand. I was hurting *so* much, so very much! I thought if I put everyone I knew in that dreadful time out of my mind I'd stop hurting. Can you understand that Mama? It was like the morphine they gave me in the hospital not to feel the pain of my wounds. Please, Mama, please forgive me! Please don't close your heart to me, don't shut me out!" She was sobbing now, tears streamed down her face and her nose was running. She took out some tissues from her bag...and she felt it – Joshua's letter.

Joshua! "Oh my God," she whispered.

She stopped sobbing, wiped her face and sat as still as the stones around her. A great calm had descended upon her; her mind was quiet, only her heart spoke – *Could you give him a chance? Hear him out?* She nodded to herself, and took the letter out. The burn mark on the left corner of the envelope, where she attempted to destroy it, suddenly felt like a monument to mercy.

She tore it open. There was just a single sheet of paper in it. She noticed a smear mark lower down on the page over the beautifully formed letters.

"Lizzie my dearest,

This is the last letter I will ever write. Before I die I must beg for your forgiveness. I am so very, very sorry for what I have done to you and our baby.

It was Bester who beat me up that night.

There it was, the long smear mark across the whole line, almost as if the tears that fell there were wiped away angrily. Lizzie lowered the letter for a moment and stared at two golden leaves chasing each other in the breeze. She frowned. Bester? She vaguely remembered the name. Oh yes, the stepbrother he had told her about. He had big fists. The bully.

He ruined my life and yours. Please understand Lizzie, after my father died I never had anyone to protect me. My mother never did when I was beaten blue and black - all she always said was: 'Joshua, what have you done! It always felt like it was all my fault. I hated her for that.

Lizzie closed her eyes and the shivers ran down her spine as she remembered her concerned words when she saw him that night, blood all over his face. Did he hear his mother's voice criticizing him? In his confused mind – perhaps it wasn't her that he attacked? Is that what he was trying to say to her when he sat by her bedside? But was that an excuse? What about the other times before she was

pregnant when he beat her when he was drunk? She
pursed her lips together and read on.

*Since that night I have never touched a drop of alcohol,
and never ever will, but it is too late to get you back and
my life is empty. It has no purpose anymore.*
    *Please can you just sometimes remember the good
times we had together and think of me kindly?*
    I will always love you,
    Joshua.

Lizzie folded the letter up and put it back in the envelope.
Her mind was already working overtime. She saw Joshua
at the hospital by her bed, his face grey and drawn. It was
just a glimpse before she had closed her eyes again –
shutting him out. Now she saw that she had only
imprisoned herself. She mused over this subtle change in
perception, this realization, for a long while. Then,
slowly, slowly she allowed the door to open and scene
after scene of their life together played itself off: their
courtship, them setting up home, the good happy times ...
and the violence – that dreadful night. That was the hard
part. In front of her was a long dark tunnel. How could
she go through it to where a light was beckoning? She
was shaking. Then she felt it: the Presence, gently
surrounding her, and she knew she could relive that night,
because she would be held.
    At last she got up. The woman was sweeping at the
gate already. She took two peace lilies from the bunch of
flowers she had bought for her mother, each one holding a
single petal over the seed head like a hand in blessing, and
laid them on his grave.
    "One for you Joshua," she said, "and one for the
memory of our marriage."
    She stood at the foot of the two graves, head bent,
hands folded over her heart.
    "Thank you Mama for forgiving me" she said. "Thank
you for praying that one day I will forgive Joshua."

She turned and looked at the two flowers on the marble slab. In time, she thought, they would wither, die, and become compost for new growth.

She felt as if she had come out of a stuffy room into the fresh air. She picked up her handbag and headed towards the gate. The wind had blown the clouds away and the sky was a deep blue made brilliant by the light of the sun. She said goodbye to the woman and walked away, on and on, until she could no longer hear the swish, swish, of her broom clearing away the dead leaves.

CHAPTER 9

Ben phoned Lizzie the morning after his conversation with Bruno.

"Lizzie, I think there's something you ought to know."

Lizzie had been apprehensive when Sarah called her to the phone. She had been reasonably peaceful inside herself since her visit to the graveyard. What was Ben going to stir up in her again now?

"My dad can move the fingers of his lame hand."

"What!! How come?"

"This is the strange bit; wait for it. Apparently Miriam had been doing some work on it with light."

"With light! What kind of light? What are you saying Ben?"

"I don't know Lizzie, I'm just telling you what my dad had told me. But this much I can tell you, he seemed like a changed man when he phoned me."

"In what way?"

"Soft, kind of gentle, and open to the things I had been trying to make him see. Like his... like he doesn't always have to be right, and in control."

Lizzie didn't know what to say. They were talking about her employer and Ben's father, how could she agree with him about Mr. Mynhard's controlling nature, but Miriam; that was another matter.

"Do you think this light Miriam is seeing is just something to do with the age she is, hormones, things like that?"

"It's possible, but then how do we account for my dad's fingers moving? And apparently he practices walking a few steps every day, three times a day? The fingers – I guess that could be just a spontaneous remission; things like that have been known to happen. But it's really his whole attitude Lizzie. In my experience, people don't just change like that over night."

Lizzie was less puzzled or bothered by the changes in Bruno; it was Miriam she was thinking of. What was happening with Miriam? Where was her little girl who confided everything in her? Ever since that strange woman from Johannesburg had that private talk with her she had become very secretive, and of late she had sensed a kind of tension between them. But with all the other things happening in her life there was no time to pay attention to that. Now, hearing this news from Ben, Lizzie knew that she had to go back. Right now; that was where her place was.

"Ben," she said, "I have to go back, I have to see what's happening with Miriam."

"And I need to see my dad, see what's brought this change in him on. I'll take a week's leave and we can drive up. Not in a rush like when we came down, that was a gruelling journey. We can take the Garden Route and have a stopover. I can book hotel rooms for us in advance. What do you say to that?"

Lizzie heard the caution in Ben's voice and his slight emphasize on the word 'rooms.' Suddenly the prospect of spending time with Ben felt good; she would like to tell him about Joshua's letter. He would be interested in that.

"Thank you Ben," she said, "let me know when we will go."

Ben and Lizzie set off from Cape Town on a fresh sunny morning a week after their conversation. Their first stop was Knysna. As a child Lizzie had been there on school trips, and she loved the place and its surrounding area.

They decided to have lunch at the Crab's Creek from where they could look across the lagoon, watching paddle cruisers steering themselves niftily through the opening between the Knysna Heads.

"Do you want to sit inside or out?" Ben asked.

"I think outside will be nice". Lizzie fingered the wooden benches, which were arranged under tall shaded trees.

They sat down and both ordered fish and local vegetables. All along the way to Knysna Lizzie had avoided talking about herself, focussing on, and enjoying the beauty of the Garden Route. Just to be able to sit back and let scene after scene come into view of the moving car: white sandy beaches, huge breaking waves, high cliffs, peculiar rock formations, and the sun flooding into the car stroking her face. It was a feast to the senses and soothing to the soul. It had been such a long time since she had seen these familiar places, and on impulse she said:

"Oh Ben, do you think after lunch we could go to Noetzie? I've never been down onto the beach. Non-whites weren't allowed to in those days. I have only ever looked down onto it from the top of the cliff. Will we have time for that? We needn't stay long."

"We can have time for whatever we want to have time for," Ben said with a soft look in his eyes, eyes that were gently stroking her face.

They parked at the cliff top and made their way down to the secluded beach that lay serene and almost deserted in front of them. Lizzie looked for the five small castles, which so fired her imagination as a child.

"Are they still privately owned houses?" she asked.

"I guess so. The wealthy who want a beach more or less to themselves don't easily give up their holiday homes."

They wet their feet in the receding waves and Lizzie quickly pulled her skirts up when an incoming wave broke at her ankles. Ben was wearing shorts and grinned at their wet foam covered legs. They walked to the end of the beach where the rocks held their own against the onslaught of the waves, and decided to climb up them so they could get a better view.

After sitting there for a while, Lizzie felt as if the sound of the breaking waves were echoing a peaceful rhythm inside her. She turned to Ben and started telling him about her visit to her mother's and Joshua's graves. She could see in Ben's eyes that he was drinking in every word. She felt so deeply listened to that she told him of the fear that washed over her when she knew she had to re-live that final attack. In the end she told him about the flowers she had laid on the grave.

Ben took her hand, his eyes full of admiration. "Brave girl," he said, then leaned over and kissed her gently on her lips.

At that moment Lizzie could not think of a more pleasant sensation to experience, and she just sat there smiling.

The waves were breaking closer to the rocks now, spattering foaming showers around so they quickly made their way down to the beach again.

It was dusk when they reached the outskirts of Port Elizabeth where Ben had booked them into a motel. Over dinner they talked about Miriam and the alleged healing, and Lizzie questioned him further.

"So she sees light and colours?"

"That's what my dad said she told him. I know there are clairvoyants who can see auras around people, and apparently they can determine their physical and emotional state by the different colours, or lack of, that they see. But we will have to talk to Miriam herself to see what is happening for *her*."

There was a softness between them, and it was as if her opening up to Ben earlier had sparked off an intimacy that was swelling like a wave. Ben started talking about his family and the death of his little sister when he was a boy. He gave a deep sigh.

"I don't think my dad ever got over that. She was the apple of his eye; he went downhill from there on. I never felt as if I was very important to him."

Lizzie saw the sadness in his bright blue eyes as she scanned his handsome face. What a kind man he was, she thought, someone one could fall in love with. The thought shocked her. Was that where she was heading?

As if Ben had tuned into the feeling he said:

"You're a very beautiful woman Lizzie, and very wise. How fortunate Miriam was to have had you to bring her up."

The air between them had become electrified and Lizzie was experiencing sensations she thought that had long been dead and buried.

"Thank you," she said simply and allowed her eyes to smile deeply into his.

He took her hand across the table and squeezed it. "Thank *you* for coming back to life."

They finished their meal and decided to take a short stroll around the motel grounds. Ben offered her his arm and she took it. A cool breeze was playing with her hair and there was a salty taste on her lips.

Back at their rooms he said: "We'll have to set off pretty early to-morrow morning. I'd like to get to the Berg before dark."

She nodded and he unlocked her door for her. Then he took her in his arms and kissed her; long enough for her to get the meaning, and she felt the joy springing up in her heart.

When she closed the door behind her she leaned against it for a while, wondering how it was that one could feel spring in the air when it was autumn already.

Miriam was very excited by the news that *Ben* was bringing Aunty Lizzie back. She could show him the painting she had made of him! What would he think of it? She wondered if she should talk to him about this thing that she seemed to be able to heal with light? She had no doubt now that Mr. Bruno could move his hand and lift it ever so slightly. Ben might know about things like that. She was still tempted to look for Internet information, perhaps Ben could help her find it? She didn't think Mr. Bruno would allow *her* to do something like that. Or, as she did before, should she just trust that the voice would guide her? She felt her body relax at this thought and intuitively she knew that the Net was not the right place for this.

She also wondered if her life would change when Aunty Lizzie was back. It was over a month since she had left. Mr. Bruno had decided that for the time being Maria should stay on, and she was pleased about that, not only because it would give her more time for her painting, but also because she genuinely liked her; the lightness around her, and her singing that made the house feel alive.

Mr. Bruno told her that the outside room where Ben would sleep should be aired and cleaned out.

"There's a lot of clutter in there, Miriam. It won't be nice for Ben to sleep in a room with boxes piled up in one corner. I would like you to sort through them and throw away rubbish: things like used wrapping paper and padded envelopes, etc. Come and show me anything you're not sure about."

Miriam took Maria with her to do the cleaning while she sorted the boxes out. It was in the third box that she came upon two rolled up canvasses. She opened the first one and her mouth fell open.

There he was: God standing on the mountain in between the two peaks, exactly as she had seen it for all those years she and Aunty Lizzie lived in the de Wit household. Who could have painted this! She looked in the corner of the painting trying to make out the signature. It was an obscure scribble, starting with a capital L followed by a capital E from where it petered out into something she couldn't make out. There was also a faded date on it.

She was about to go and consult Mr. Bruno when she remembered that there was another rolled up canvas. *Better take that one with me too*, she thought.

"I'll be back in a minute," she said to Maria.

Mr. Bruno was massaging his hand when she found him on the veranda, something he was doing now all the time when he was sitting unoccupied.

"I found these paintings in a box Mr. Bruno," she held the two rolls up.

"Paintings?" He looked puzzled, his frown folding into its carved out path, then: "Ah yes – I'd forgotten about them."

Miriam rolled the one of God on the mountain open and held it up to him.

"Who painted this? I can't make the name out."

Mr. Bruno looked at the signature. "Yes, I remember, a guy called Erasmus, same man who sculpted the hand," he pointed to the marble creation on the table.

Something big stirred in Miriam. The man, who made the hand that she had so often stroked lovingly, especially when she felt lonely, had painted her beloved mountain on the other side! She started to unroll the other canvas, but before she got very far she suddenly knew what she had in her hand, and her heart thumped as if it would jump out of her rib cage.

There it was: a portrait of a young Zulu girl. Fastened around her head was a bright coloured orange scarf harmonizing with the smiling brown eyes. The full moist lips catching the sunshine, was giving it a sensuality that was almost palpable. And at the bottom, just above the artist signature, one word: LOKKIE.

Miriam felt her legs giving way under her and the last she heard as she slumped into the nearest chair was Mr. Bruno's booming voice.

"Maria! Maria! Come here quickly!"

When she came too, both Maria and Filamon were on the veranda and her face felt wet. Cinnamon was pushing against her legs as if urging her to come back and Honey was licking her toes.

"Help her to her room Maria, let her lie down" There was deep concern in Mr. Bruno's voice.

Maria came to help her up but she waved her away.

"I *don't* want to lie down! I want to see that portrait again. Give it to me!" She was holding a demanding hand out to him.

162

"Miriam?" The confusion was in Mr. Bruno's voice, but she hardly heard him.

"Give her to me, let me look at my mother!"

"Your mother! What are you talking about?"

Miriam snatched the canvas from him, and unrolled it slowly, taking every inch of it in, lost in a world of her own. As if a spell had been cast over them, no one moved, not even the dogs. At last she tore her eyes away from the portrait and looked at Mr. Bruno.

"Hester said my mother was a Zulu girl whose name was Lokkie, and that my father had painted a portrait of her."

Bruno took a deep breath, "Wow!" He shifted his lame limb a few inches up his lap and stared at Miriam as the connection slowly sank in. At last he spoke.

"Well Miriam, then we must have it framed so that you can hang it in your room."

The fight fled from Miriam. "Thank you Mr. Bruno, thank you *very* much." She had caught the slight movement of his hand and her eyes went to the solid marble hand on the table. "Then the man who made *that,* must be my father. Is he still alive?"

"I don't know Miriam – Ben might know, he visits art galleries."

Miriam rolled the picture up carefully and handed it to Mr. Bruno. She turned to Maria.

"We'd better get that room done."

The sun was just setting when, from her bedroom window, Miriam saw Ben's car crawling up the dirt road. Her first impulse was to rush out, but suddenly she felt awkward and held back. So much has happened to her in the weeks since she last saw them that she felt shy, almost as if they were strangers to her, or she to them. When Aunty Lizzie got out of the car, the feeling became even stronger. She had never seen light around her, but now she had a lovely pink aura and her eyes shone, lighting up her face. She looked beautiful. She saw Ben as he walked around the car to the boot, and it hit her hard: there was a similar pinkish glow around him. So that was it; they were in love.

She sat down on her bed unable to move. Mr. Bruno was out there and the dogs were thumping their tails about, and she knew they were expecting her to rush out too, but she couldn't. She heard them come into the house and Aunty Lizzie calling out:

"Miriam! Where are you? We're here!" Then there was a knock on the door.

"Miriam!"

She got up and opened the door. Aunty Lizzie was standing in front of her, shining, expecting her to throw her arms around her, and all she could do was to move forward and give her a cold peck on the check. She saw the hurt and bewilderment on Aunty Lizzie's face, and she felt terrible. Inside her a darkness had got hold of her.

Ben came through carrying Aunty Lizzie's suitcase and saw her.

"Miriam! Good to see you."

He put the suitcase down and gave her a hug. She responded slightly, almost as if against her will. He didn't seem to have noticed her reluctance, and took the suitcase to Aunty Lizzie's room. Aunty Lizzie turned away from her and followed him.

Miriam went back into her room and locked the door. She could see a thick blackness in her body as clearly as she had seen it in Mr. Bruno's hand, before the light lifted it out. She was trembling, hiding her face in her hands when the voice came, calm and without judgement:

"This is what jealousy looks like."

She felt sick. She and the voice had been here before, but to *see* it, not only having the word spoken – that was horrendous. There was no light in her, none at all! This is like death, she thought. How can I live with this?

There was a hesitant knock on the door.

"Miriam," Maria's melodious voice was apologetic, "please to come and help me with the food. I not know to make the sauce."

Miriam opened the door slightly. Maria stood before her vibrant, her smiling face displaying a row of white teeth. The contrast between herself and Maria shocked Miriam even more. She knew she couldn't go out.

"Maria," she said, "I'm not feeling well, please tell the master I don't want supper, I want to be left alone."

She closed the door on the astonished Maria and locked it. At the window she stood staring at the dusk spreading its gloom all over the garden and it seemed to her that even the air was heavy and stifling.

The eagle... could it, even at this late hour, come to her? Her ears were cocked, but she knew there would be no comfort from there. She hated the dense darkness in her body, and wanted to scream at it to go away, leave her alone, but the more she tried to rid herself of it, the thicker and more menacing it became. It's all Aunty Lizzie's fault, she thought, if she had never come to live here, Ben would have...

She caught her breath as she realized what she was thinking, extreme tiredness washed over her whole body. She went to her bed and sat down, viewing herself with that inner eye that saw the putrid darkness emanating from Mr. Bruno's hand. She remembered her disgust and fear; fear that she might be contaminated by it. The voice spoke to her then; what did it say? Oh yes: it told her to focus on the Light. *But there is no light in me,* her thoughts argued, *only darkness, I can see only darkness.* The words of the voice came back to her memory: *You give the darkness power by focusing on it,* it said, something like that, yes it did. *But... I mean, how can I ...* Tears overwhelmed her. "Help me, please help me," she sobbed; and through the sobs a thought wiggled itself into her consciousness: to focus on the lovely pink glow she saw around Aunty Lizzie when she got out of the car. Her first impulse was to resist: *No, it was she who caused all this misery in me!*

But deep down there was no kidding herself. She knew her feelings had nothing to do with Aunty Lizzie, it all belonged to her, and it was hers to hang on to or to let go of.

She blew her nose, put her pyjamas on and crawled into bed; exhaustion mercifully took her into the oblivion of sleep.

She woke up in the night with a need to go to the loo. The clock said ten to twelve. When she got back into bed she was wide-awake. Sleep had fled from her and she felt desperately unhappy. With a heavy, dull feeling she thrashed around for another hour, and then quietly got up. She sneaked into the living area and the dogs thumped their tails in their baskets. Cinnamon got up and came to her.

"Down Cinny," she whispered, "Back!" she pointed a finger, "Back into your basket." Cinnamon obeyed and she quietly unlocked the French doors.

A fresh breeze was rustling the shrubs, which shed golden leaves on the lawn that Filamon had cut the day before. A half moon was stealing from cloud to cloud, lighting up the table on the veranda; then abandoning it to darkness. It was when it peeped out from behind a particularly dark cloud that Miriam saw its light streaming onto the hand, allowing its marble to gleam in the darkness like a beacon.

She sat down and slipped her hand into its supplicating shape. Her fingers entwined with its fingers. Slowly she stroked it, rhythmically; and after a while a peacefulness started to fold itself around her, transporting her to a place inside herself that carried no knowledge of things like jealousy or hatred.

She was startled by a sound behind her and turned around. Aunty Lizzie was opening the French doors wearing a thick fluffy dressing gown that she had not seen before. All around her was that lovely pink glow which Miriam had seen when she got out of the car; but now, in the near darkness of the night it seemed like a lifeline thrown out to her. Aunty Lizzie sat down next to her and smiled.

Spontaneously Miriam returned the smile.

"It was my father who made this hand," she said as she kept on stroking, "and in dark times like this, he holds my hand and helps me."

As if the words dislodged something that had got stuck in her, Miriam's shoulders started shaking. She let go of the hand and almost against her will threw both her arms around Aunty Lizzie.

"I love you so much Aunty Lizzie!" she sobbed.

She felt Aunty Lizzie's strong firm arms securely around her, rocking her like a baby. The half moon drifted across the sky past a few twinkling stars and smiled at the two entwined figures, each dissolving their respective grief in Love.

Lizzie had been concerned when Maria brought the news that Miriam was not well and she wanted to go to her straight away, but Bruno held his hand up.

"Leave her Lizzie, there's things I have to tell you first." He put his teacup down. "I think Maria might need your help with the supper, we can talk when she's gone home."

When Lizzie heard the story of the portrait – Miriam's mother – she could feel that old familiar sensation, which was always lurking in some dark corner inside her, showing its ugly face again. Bruno's voice was floating over her, she heard his words but they were meaningless to her.

"So you see she's had a shock; and at her age too. I think we must let her have her privacy and let her have time to sort things out by herself."

Ben was nodding in agreement and Lizzie felt the amicable warmth between father and son, which surprised her after what Ben had told her in Port Elizabeth. She felt excluded, alone and deprived.

Ben's voice interrupted her thoughts. "You look tired Lizzie; it's been a long drive. If you want to go to bed, I'll clear up here and see to my dad's needs."

Lizzie struggled with the sense of feeling dismissed, yet was grateful for the escape. She needed to be by herself as much as Miriam did.

In her room she undressed and got into bed, but sleep eluded her. So this was why Miriam gave her such a cool reception. She had seen what her mother, her real mother looked like; and the old refrain came into her head: *How can I compete with Miriam's mother for her love?* Miriam, her Miriam, was in the room next to her, only a thin wall separating them, and yet she might have been ten million miles away. Her thoughts were like a ball of entangled wool, and she was unable to sort them out. She tossed and turned until tiredness from the long journey took her into sleep.

Something woke her up but she didn't know what it was. She felt as if she had been sleeping for an eternity, convinced that it was nearly morning, but when she turned the light on and looked at her watch it was just after one o'clock. She got up and put her new dressing gown on to go to the bathroom, but when she passed Miriam's room she noticed the door ajar. Very quietly she opened it and peeped inside. Miriam's bed was empty. She went to the bathroom; that was empty too. Feeling alarm rising within her, she went into the living area. Through the French doors she saw Miriam, sitting by the long table slightly bent over. Relief washed over her, and as she stood there watching her for a moment she felt her deep, deep love for the lonely little figure out there in the dark.

She knew she could never abandon her.

Bruno and Ben sat at the table after Lizzie had left. They discussed Ben's work and the impact his further education had on it.

"Industrial psychology has a great future," Ben said. "Big business has woken up to it. They can see the financial benefits for themselves in it when their staff are experiencing job satisfaction. This year and a half I spent on getting my Masters is paying off handsomely now."

As Ben was elaborating on the influence thoughts, feelings and beliefs have on people's happiness Bruno was amazed at how interesting he found it all. Yet at the same time there was something niggling inside him. He remembered the demeaning remarks he had made about psychology and he now felt uncomfortable about the attitude he had then. Why had he been so against it? Was Ben right? *Was* he afraid of his own emotions so deeply buried?

When Ben had finished talking about his work, he got up and cleared the table; then he brought two cups of coffee in. The atmosphere was congenial and Bruno felt relaxed and open, so when Ben said, "Dad, I can't get over the change in you, and so suddenly too," he smiled and toyed with the idea of telling Ben about the dreams. He decided not to, for now at least. He wasn't ready yet to expose the shrivelled-up legs to Ben's psychological scrutiny.

"Miriam is a very talented young girl," he said instead. "Something radiates from her that is quite wholesome, and she is very intelligent."

Ben saw an opening. "That she certainly is, and she is High School age now. I guess it will become increasingly difficult for you to teach her the variety of lessons she would need for her matriculation."

Bruno stiffened visibly. Once again it was Ben who touched on something he had refused to face. He needed Miriam. He could not let her go. He felt convinced that he would recover at least some of his mobility if she were to continue her work with him. He needed her presence in his life.

"I've been thinking of you a lot lately," Ben continued. "There has been such a lot of new developments in science over the last years. I believe that the latest methods in physiotherapy and occupational therapy could move your recovery on considerably, and what with Miriam's work on you – I mean such a combination, eh..." Ben was struggling. The stakes were high.

"What are you saying Ben?" Bruno's frown was back. "There are no physiotherapist or occupational therapists here, you know *that*."

"Exactly Dad," Ben was getting his breath back. "But there are in Cape Town, *and* there is a first class High School there too, one in which you spent years of your life building its reputation."

Bruno's eyes were big under his frown as he stared at Ben.

"You mean, you mean we should..."

"Why not Dad? You don't have to stay here, you and Miriam and Lizzie could move back there."

Lizzie. Yes Lizzie, Bruno thought. She had said she would come back, but how could he know for sure, now that her circumstances had changed? And of course Ben was right; he could not give Miriam the education she needed much longer. He felt the fear contracting his heart. To go back to the place where he had lost so much: his health, his profession, and his authority. And yet... if he could gain some of his health back... a hundred thousand thoughts were churning around in his head; possibilities were flickering through. He was excited and he saw the lame hand trembling slightly. *Before now it couldn't even tremble*, he thought. *Anxiety might not be such a bad thing if it means the difference between stagnation and moving forward.*

"Ben," he said, "it's certainly an idea: let's chew it over."

Ben got up. He placed his hand on Bruno's shoulder.

"Dad, if you decide to make this change in your life, you can count on my support one hundred percent."

Bruno nodded. He looked at his watch. "There's an interesting programme on Fanie's Island that I'd like to watch, showing now, will you watch it with me?"

Ben turned to switch the television on, but also to hide his broad spontaneous smile.

When Ben said at breakfast the next morning, "Miriam I'm dying to see that portrait of the other me that has been kept such a secret!" she beamed.

"I'll show you soon as we've finished eating."

She was sitting close to Aunty Lizzie; ashamed of the dark thoughts she had harboured the night before. The light was back in her, and watching the pink aura around Aunty Lizzie made her feel loving towards everyone. She noticed that some change of colour had crept into Mr. Bruno's face at Ben's words. It had darkened and she saw him hiding his hand. She remembered his shock when he first saw Ben's frightened eyes in the picture.

After breakfast Mr. Bruno went straight to his room and she saw him closing his door when she went to fetch the painting. When she came back, Ben was alone. Aunty Lizzie was helping Maria. She spread the picture out in front of him.

"Is that true Miriam?" he said after a while, "Did I really look that scared?"

She nodded. "You looked like a lost child."

Ben rubbed his chin and mouth, reflecting.

"When was that, Miriam?"

"At supper the night before Good Friday."

Ben looked at Miriam   as he recalled the gloomy tension around the table that night and shook his head.

"You *really* are very talented Miriam; exceptionally perceptive."

Miriam felt the light in her expanding as she looked at the brightness around Ben. He scanned the painting for a long time. At last he said.

"We'll have to get you into Art School."

"No, I want to go to medical school when I'm old enough. I want to become a doctor."

Ben looked at Miriam intently. "You want to become a doctor?"

She nodded. "I want to help heal people."

"With light?"

"How do you know that!" she was shocked.

"My dad told me what you've been doing to his hand."

"Oh. It wasn't really me Ben, the light just comes, flows through me, and I just hold it. I want to know what is where in our bodies so that the light and I can... well, ah... I don't really know," she felt herself floundering, "it is the light that does the work Ben," she ended almost pleadingly.

Ben looked at her for a long time. "You are an extraordinary being," he said at last. "I think the light that you work with, or works through you as you said, heals more than just the body. How proud I would have been if *you* were my little sister."

The scales fell from Miriam's eyes and she saw in front of her a mature man, nearly three times her age. All at once she understood the kind of love she felt for Ben. Relief washed over her like a cleansing waterfall and she felt almost overwhelmed by it. She knew she could never lose Ben's love.

She heard Mr. Bruno's wheelchair squeaking down the passage and got up. She felt a deep need to be outside, to be looking at the mountain, to search for the eagle, and to see the autumn colours dancing in the breeze.

Bruno pulled his chair up to the table where Ben was still sitting, staring at his portrait. He cleared his throat and Ben looked up.

"Ben," he said pointing to the portrait, "I am so sorry. What can I do to make up for this?"

To his amazement he saw moisture springing up in Ben's blue eyes, and he thought, *how lovely they look.*

Ben's voice was cracking when he answered. "Forgive yourself, Dad. Just forgive yourself. That's the best thing you can do."

Bruno felt the last remnants of his rigid defences crumble as, in his mind, Ben's words echoed the voice of the black clad man of the dream: "All our sins are forgiven."

Bruno had asked Ben to take Miriam to the picture framers in Harrysmith so that she could choose a frame and mount for Lokkie's portrait. Miriam's eyes were sparkling, laughing with joy when she got into the car with him. Soon they had left the mountain behind, and the rolling hills of KwaZulu-Natal were displaying a swell of green carpet on both sides of the snaking road.

"There's some very good picture framing shops in Cape Town," Ben said, "They're like artists in their own right, let's hope this one can do justice to the picture."

Miriam sighed. "We have so little here." She was silent for a moment. "Except for the beauty of the mountain of course, and this," she swept her hand across the windscreen to take in the expanse of nature displayed in front of them.

"Yes, it is very beautiful," Ben said, "but Cape Town is very beautiful too. You've not been there Miriam?"

She shook her head.

"I can just see you painting some angle of The Twelve Apostles, the view from Camps Bay perhaps."

Miriam sighed again.

"It would be so lovely to see all that. Perhaps now that Aunty Lizzie has a house there she might visit her family sometime and take me along for a holiday."

"Would you like to live there, Miriam?"

She thought for a moment as in her mind's eye she saw her rock god, silhouetted against the sky, the clouds riding like chariots above his head. She had a sudden sense of loss as she realized that she could never go back to that innocent time again. But here, now, there was *this* side of the mountain, which she had come to love too. And her Eagle.

"Maybe," she said, and after a while, "It can get so very lonely here."

"There's a well equipped hospital there where the first ever heart transplant operation was done. If you want to become a doctor, Cape Town would be a good place to be."

Miriam sat up. "Really? I mean…"

"There's an excellent high school there too. You would need a good education if you want to get into medical school."

Miriam was all ears as Ben went on extolling the benefits of Cape Town, and ended with:

"And of course the art galleries are a feast, the private ones as well as the public ones."

Listening to Ben in the intimacy of the speeding car Miriam, for the first time, felt a need to tell someone the story that Hester had told her about her mother; all the sad details, the tin of money, her mother's naïve intention of buying a house, and finally the brutal murder. She knew she could open up to Ben. She took a deep breath and it all just poured out of her – everything. She felt that she was being listened to as she'd never been listened to before.

"Ben," she said when she had finished, her voice hushed as if she was entering a cathedral, "I need to find my father. Please will you help me?"

Ben slowed the car as he looked at Miriam's pleading green eyes set in the oval face, the black frizzy curls swaying in the wind.

"I will Miriam," he said, his voice matching her reverent tone. "We know his surname, we know he's an artist: it might take some time but the Internet could help." His voice dropped another tone as he made his commitment. "I will help you, I promise."

Thoughts about relocating to Cape Town, even if only temporarily, had been occupying Bruno's mind since Ben had broached the subject. He had opened the little bureau in his room and made a thorough study of his financial affairs: his savings, his investments, and his properties. It was possible to keep the smallholding on and rent a house in Cape Town, see how that worked out first. There was gratitude in his heart for what he and Kate had inherited from their mother and grandmother, and he had made some lucrative, well thought through, investments with it. Money would not be a problem, and he had Ben's promise of physical support. But how would Miriam and Lizzie feel about it? He asked Lizzie to join him on the veranda after his rest so that he could discuss it with her.

She sat opposite him, dressed, not in her uniform as he had expected, but in an olive green jersey cloth dress that sat snugly around her body; a dress that he had never seen her wear before. Her hair was brushed out, cascading down her shoulders and around her face, cut into a new style that suited her well. So that was why she was in town for such a long time this morning, he thought. He had assumed she had visited Sunda and Abdullah on her way back. She looked radiant in a way he had never seen her look before. She was stroking the dogs that sat in front of her like two live statues, fondling their ears. Little episodes of interactions between her and Ben flashed through his mind.

My God, he thought, *how could I have been so blind, so absorbed in my healing sessions with Miriam, and thinking through the plan that Ben had proposed, that I didn't see what was happening?*

Suddenly the reality hit him: a romantic relationship - a marriage perhaps? The possibility of having a coloured grandchild one day! Good heavens! It was one thing having a cosy domestic relationship with two coloured people in his household with him holding the reins but...He swallowed as the inconsistency glared at him: how was it that in his affections he could think of Miriam in terms of Amelie, yet he stalled in front of having a coloured grandchild? He shifted on his chair as if wanting to escape from the grip of the merciless thought: *indoctrination - so subtle, it was almost like taking it in with his mother's milk.* He put his hand in front of his mouth, before slowly moving it to one side, as if wiping away something distasteful. *What a legacy! Not only what had been passed on from his ancestors – but from a whole nation, a country!*

Lizzie's voice broke his reverie. "You wanted to see me Mr. Mynhard?"

He cleared his throat as if to make way for what he had to swallow. It was hard, too hard for dealing with in this moment; and he escaped into the thought: *nothing might come of it; it might only be an enjoyable romance.*

"Yes Lizzie," he smiled. "I wanted to ask you if you would have any objections if you, Miriam and I moved down to Cape Town."

Lizzie's eyes went wide, as if she just couldn't believe her ears.

"Objections! Mr. Mynhard! How could I have objections? And our Miriam, she can go to school there amongst children of her own age!"

Bruno lowered his head – yet another one of his thoughtless, selfish actions. He thought of his anger over the possible disturbance of his comfortable routine, not so very many weeks ago. But Ben's voice was still fresh in his memory: 'Forgive yourself Dad', and somehow it was sustaining him.

A deep sense of gratitude descended on him: gratitude towards Miriam and her light, and the black clad man, which he now felt sure, had something to do with that same light. The light that none of them really understood but which nevertheless did its work. *Much, much work to be done yet,* he thought, *but I am willing.*

On impulse he said, "Lizzie, please will you call me Bruno from now on?"

He saw in Lizzie's eyes, as she smiled shyly, that she understood what he meant by that.

"Sure Mr. Mynhard, I mean…" her laughter rippled from the veranda across the garden like a clear bell.

"Yes, Bruno," she said firmly.

Their eyes met.

"Thank you Lizzie."

Filamon came to the veranda. "Yebo Master." He gave his familiar salute. "The red hen, Master, not good, head like this," he bent his forefinger pointing down.

"Since when?"

"This morning when I bring the food, not eating."

"Thank you Filamon, I'll come and have a look at her later."

Filamon, Bruno thought: he'd have to find a job for him. He had been working here for a long time. Work was not easy to find, but he was determined not to leave Filamon stranded, even if he had to keep him on just to look after the place for a while.

"It will be a wrench for me, Lizzie, leaving this lovely place," he said looking at the jagged peaks of the mountain, wondering whether they would be wearing their snow-hats again this winter when he wouldn't be here to see them.

CHAPTER 10

Leonard Erasmus sat staring at the enormous waves rolling into the bay, puffing themselves up into giant castles only to be smashed a minute later on the sand, turning into nothing but froth. For some reason they reminded him of his father and how, as a little boy, he hated Sundays.

It was the worst day of the week, the day he had to wear his long pants in the sweltering heat, a buttoned-up shirt and a jacket. Worst of all, he had to sit still (*no fiddling*) on those hard church benches for one whole hour while the preacher's voice droned on and on. Standing up to sing psalms was a brief break from the torture, especially when his father's strict attention on him slackened as he tried to make his strong sonorous voice heard above those of the congregation. He was proud of his voice, and when he couldn't sing, he talked. Yet his talking voice bore no relation to his singing voice. It was stilted, one wooden sentence after another, no flow, no spontaneity. He had a habit of repeating people's names: *Now that bull, Leonard, is not one of the best on the show, if you look at Dan Jansen's bull, Leonard,* ... and on and on with another 'Leonard' or two thrown in before his arrogantly authoritative discourse ended.

In a way it was a relief to him when his father was appointed church elder and took his place in the row of honour with the others. Leonard had watched them from the safe distance behind other wooden benches where his father could not see him twisting his handkerchief round and round until he had made a swan out of it. He would nudge his mother to look and she would smile at his creation. It was much better sitting just with her.

As he got older and bored of making swans, he studied the honoured front row. There they sat, looking like pawns on a chessboard: dark suited men, each wearing a pious face. Next to his father was the dour, grey-faced primary school teacher with his narrow forehead sloping into his bushy eyebrows. On his other side was the high school teacher who, his father had said, might yet be headmaster one day. His long red face with anxious eyes was pasted firmly above his dark tie and starched shirt collar. Two schoolteachers ... even as a little boy he could see his father's satisfaction in being placed next to them. "I might only be a farmer Elizabeth," he would say to his mother, "but one day soon, I might be a member of parliament."

To Leonard, church was a stark, stuffy place, literally and figuratively. No statues, no paintings, not even flowers – apparently God had said in the Ten Commandments that there should be no graven images where one worshipped Him. It wasn't that he didn't believe in God. He did – always had. To him it seemed inconceivable not to believe in God. It was more than a belief, it was a *knowing*. If there were no God, there could be no Leonard. To him they were inseparable, but in this church, amongst these people, it was hard for him to fathom the God that the preacher was shouting about from the pulpit. That was why the acceptance of the creed of the church they belonged to, which was forced upon him, made him feel like a traitor: betraying this caring God, the inner core of himself.

He remembered those torturous months of studying this belief system set out in a series of Questions and Answers which had to be worked through Sunday after Sunday with one elder or another. They interpreted the answers and applied them to their lives, but Leonard felt they had no bearing whatsoever – neither on his life, nor on the way his thoughts ran. To him the pinnacle of humiliation came on the Sunday of their confirmation. They filed in, twenty of them to take their oath, and there he stood at the age of sixteen in front of the pulpit, dressed in a suit, collar and dark tie – his first. He felt as if he was choking. He thought that it might be like this if one were marrying the wrong girl, a loveless affair while his true love was longing for him outside this barren building.

Leonard often wondered how it could have happened that a gentle, beautiful woman like his mother got herself married to a man like his father. How was it that she could leave a pleasant seaside town in the East Cape to live with him in a flat Free State town?

His mother always had, and even now still had, the kind of beauty that you simply didn't analyse: nose, eyes, hair… People just looked into those sparkling green eyes and saw an exceptionally beautiful woman. Every one could see that. Thinking of it now, he realized that she must have been very lonely all those years. It wasn't so much living on the farm that caused it. On the farm her days were full and, to her, interesting. She grew medicinal herbs and made a remedy for almost any ailment, or so she said. He, however, knew there was more to it than that. Herbal remedies were acceptable to his dad, only just, and the town's people were open to it. She used it as a smoke screen for what she really did. She let him into her secret one day when he was poring over her latest potion, thinking her very clever.

"That's not what helped Aunty Bessie's gout."

He was shocked.

"It wasn't? What was it then, she said she didn't take the doctor's medicine?"

"You see my Love, the thing that really heals is light."

"So you lie to the people when you give them your medicine!"

"No, not at all. Everything, everything in existence has a sparkle of light in it, so that helps and it helps me."

"How?"

"It gives me a chance to work with the light on them. Like when I rub this ointment into Aunty Bessie's feet I call upon the light and direct it to where I see the dark shrivelled up cells in the bones and tissues. That's what helps her."

He was only twelve then and he preferred his mates to think of his mother as the town's herbalist rather than boasting to them about some weird healing with light that she said she did. How isolated she must have felt amongst those narrow-minded people who could, at the drop of a hat, or rather a word of disapproval from the preacher, have started a witch hunt against her, and ruined his dad's political aspirations. Perhaps that was the reason she took the role of the meek obedient wife.

But not in all things.

The time came when there was no denying his talent. Yet his dad still tried to brush it off.

"Yeah, not bad Leonard, but I can tell you this, to have a real standing in the world Leonard, politics is a much better bet."

He saw his mother lips tighten but she said nothing. She couldn't fight his father's pomposity with words, so she went out and bought him a beautiful piece of marble. That triggered a storm.

"Spending all that money Elizabeth! And that on something that will only strengthen his fancy ideas!"

His mother had planted her neat feet firmly in front of his bulk.

"Leonard is a talented artist, and I will encourage him in it."

Neither he nor his father had ever seen her like that. Her eyes were flashing fire, and there was a determination around her mouth that made it clear that she would not budge an inch. His dad was shocked and he could see the fleshy lips slightly quivering as the shifty eyes headed for the carpet. He muttered something about 'honouring the traditions of the forefathers' and 'tried and tested professions', but she had turned her back on him and her gait spoke volumes.

He could feel undercurrents rippling through their lives, destroying the old order.

The idea came to him to carve that precious material into a hand. He wondered why, and as he sat chipping away he felt as if the material was coming alive in him, becoming a part of him. The phrase jumped into his head: *The hand of God.* He put his heart and soul into the sculpting; seeing it as some sort of atonement for the betrayal he felt at his confirmation. Slowly, slowly as the work took shape, firm ideas formed in his mind. There were two more school terms left before the end of his high school years – he would *not* go to Pretoria or Potchefstroom, the two universities his father had in mind for him: "Good solid institutions with Calvinistic values Leonard, where you could study law or theology Leonard, both respected qualifications Leonard, which will give you a standing in society".

He passed his matric first class and announced that he was taking a gap year, going to Europe to see the world and to study art in England. His dad's face was red with anger and his forefinger bobbed up and down with every threat that he uttered. His mother did not utter a word, but he felt her presence like a rock behind him and when his dad played his trump card, "Not a cent will you get from me, Leonard, not a cent, do you understand me Leonard?" his mother spoke.

"You can have whatever is in my savings account Lennie."

Lennie – her using the name she sometimes called him as a little boy in tender moments between them – did it. It gave him the strength to defy his father and take the chance of making the trip on a shoestring.

To save money he decided to hitchhike his way up north to the airport. It occurred to him that if he first branched off east through KwaZulu-Natal, to take in the Drakensberg mountain range, painting as he went, he might be able to sell some canvasses and perhaps take some away with him. Something to sell while he was abroad. He took the marble hand with him even though it was heavy in his rucksack, but the very weight of it was a reminder, a kind of confirmation, that what he was doing was what his soul had dictated.

He had never been to those magnificent mountains before, and when he stood, awe struck, in a deep vale surrounded by their majestic presence, he felt as insignificant as an ant. But he held onto the awareness of the weight of the hand in his rucksack and he said to himself: *I am in the hand of God.*

A young girl with an orange scarf tied around her head, wearing a short summer dress of faded green cotton, came walking up the winding footpath, swinging her slender body rhythmically to the sound of her chanting. She was carrying a bundle of firewood tied together in one hand and an urn in the other. The contours and movement of her body plucked at the artist in him and brought forth sweet feelings like music produced from plucking the strings of a guitar. He stepped out of the footpath and she passed by, eyes cast down demurely. He watched her as she walked away and felt uplifted by the beautiful lines of her body disappearing down a low hill. He sat down and made a few sketches of her figure from memory, and then took a sandwich from the container of food the kind lady had packed for him at his last lodge. The smell of dried-up animal dung drifted towards him on the breeze – goats perhaps? Or cows? When the slight gust hushed, the wild flowers reigned supreme, offering their perfume to the mountain; and to mankind. He felt totally at peace as he scanned the rugged peaks of the mountain, lit up by a glorious sun exposing every nook and cranny. Then he saw it: a peculiar upright rock standing there like a man posing for a painting. He put his half-eaten sandwich down, took out his easel and paints and set to work. He finished just as the sun withdrew its light, and packed up his belongings.

When he put his rucksack on his back he saw a long shadow climbing up the low hill trailing the girl with the orange scarf behind it. As she came close to him he smiled:

"Is there anywhere near here that I can get water?"

She stopped and looked at him; soft smiling eyes.

"I go there now. You walk after me."

He followed her, his eyes stroking her shining brown legs, travelling up to the shapely buttocks, slim waist and slender shoulders. They came to a clear stream running from some rocks like a small waterfall. She bent down and filled her urn.

"What's your name," he asked as he filled his plastic bottle.

"Lokkie," she said shyly, but didn't ask for his name.

"Where do you live Lokkie?"

She pointed in the direction from which they had come.

"Is there anywhere here that I can pitch my tent?"

She nodded. "Walk after me."

When they reached a cluster of three huts the sun had withdrawn its spotlight completely from the rock where the man with his flowing beard stood on the mountain. They were greeted by the sound of children shouting and laughing, but he saw no adults around. Four children dressed in rags came running up to them and spoke to the girl in Zulu. She smiled and pinched a thin cheeky looking boy playfully by the nose.

"Whose children are they?" he asked.

"It's from my sister and my auntie's daughter."

"Do they live here?"

She nodded. "But not now, now they work in the big city for the money."

"And you look after them?"

She nodded again and looked at him shyly, her eyes shining, her full lips slightly moist.

"So where can I pitch my tent?"

She pointed to the far hut. "You can sleep there, is empty."

"And the children, where do they sleep?"

"In this one, with me."

She walked ahead of him and opened the door. Stale air greeted him as he went inside and put his belongings down in the empty hut. He wondered why there was no furniture, no bed, nothing, and she answered him as if she had heard his question.

"The bed gone to my other aunty, will come back when this one come back," she tapped on the hut with her finger as if it represented its owner.

That evening he joined her around the open fire in the middle of the cluster and she offered him some of the crumble porridge she fed to the children. He took out a slab of chocolate from his pocket and shared it out between them all. The children shrieked with delight, clapping their hands twice before opening them to receive the precious gift. They smiled at him as they danced around the fire.

Then he asked the big question.

"Tomorrow, please will you let me paint a portrait of you Lokkie?"

She gasped; eyes large with surprise then hid her face in her hands and giggled with excitement. Her pleasure charmed him and he felt like taking her in his arms.

That night alone in the airless hut lit only by two candles, he made a few sketches as he remembered her leading him to the clear mountain stream: the lean brown legs, the shapely buttocks swinging from side to side, the head slightly to the one side. He had a vision of expanding it into a large canvas once he reached England. He felt sure it would sell there for a good price.

The next morning he was awakened by singing, children's voices, and her voice. When he came out of the hut he saw her stirring crumble porridge in a large black pot hanging over the fire. The children came up to him looking at him expectantly, but he had no more chocolate.

He worked at her portrait all that day. She sat for him an hour here and an hour there in between her household chores, but he continued without her formal pose, often just watching her graceful movements. Just after midday they went down with urns and his bottles to the stream for water and they picked up some firewood along the way. It felt cosy, a kind of pleasant domestic situation.

"What your name?" she said when they came to the stream cascading from the rocks.

Somehow he felt that Leonard did not fit the carefree atmosphere; too formal, and without thinking he said "Lennie," the abbreviation his father despised.

"Lennie!" She laughed, "I like."

He felt his heart expand as he looked into her gentle eyes, and spontaneously he took her into his arms and kissed her full lips. Her body yielded and he felt the soft breasts against his chest.

They both knew that she would spend the night in his hut when the children were asleep.

He stayed two more days, in the evenings telling her about his plans to become a great artist one day, and that he was on his way to England to learn more.

"Ayish, very far," she said.

He nodded, "And I will be away for a long time, but I will show them your picture and everyone will like it and I will remember you by it. Look, I have written your name on it, here, 'Lokkie'." She looked pleased and crept close into his arms.

He left the huts at daybreak on the third morning and headed out of the valley up onto the mountain slopes. Once on the main road he hitched a few lifts through some small towns where he bought provisions. He had shared his dehydrated food with Lokkie and the children; a staple diet of porridge did not suit him. With his supplies replenished he walked along the main road listening for the sound of a motor vehicle, but the roads were quiet and he must have walked for about five miles before through the trees he spotted a house just off the main road. He decided to see if he could sell some of the paintings he had made on his travels so far. Outside on a large veranda an electric buggy was parked and a honey coloured pup came to greet him with courageous baby barks interspersed with attempted growling.

A man with a walking stick came out of the house. "Good afternoon," Leonard said.

The man nodded, "Good afternoon."

Leonard held out his hand, "Erasmus, Leonard Erasmus."

They shook hands, "Mynhard."

"Pleased to meet you Mr. Mynhard."

He felt the suspicion in the older man's attitude and bent down to fondle the puppy's ears. "I've made some paintings of this beautiful part of our country, I wondered if you'd care to see if there's something you might like."

"Can do," the man said with half-hearted interest.

Leonard took out the painting of the man-rock and spread it out on the table. Immediately he sensed interest.

"That's near where my sister lives. You can see that rock from their house." He looked at it for a while. "That's pretty good," and after a while, "any more?"

Leonard took out some work he had done before he entered The Berg, but there was no interest. He felt a need for more approval and took out the portrait of Lokkie. There was interest, even admiration. He felt flattered and excited.

"I do sculpting too."

"Oh yes? Anything to hand?"

Leonard smiled at the coincidence, laid the marble hand on the table and stood back, keenly observing the man's reactions. Suddenly the air had become electrified.

"My God!" He was fingering the hand over and over again. "How much do you want for this?"

Leonard stood in shock. He had never intended selling it and said so, but that seemed to fire the man's desire for the object.

"Look man, I can pay, you just name your price."

Leonard shook his head. "This piece of work is very personal to me, I've put my heart and soul into it and…"

187

"Yes, I can see that. Tell you what; I'll take those two paintings off you if you let me have the sculpture. How about ten thousand Rand for the three."

Leonard's head was swimming. Ten thousand Rand! What a wonderful recognition for his work! It was very gratifying but still he shook his head. The man looked disappointed and for the first time he noticed his long frown.

"Sorry Mr. Mynhard, the paintings are one thing, but the hand, I mean the marble alone…

"You must be tired, let's have a cup of tea."

It was a command. He shouted an instruction in Zulu and Leonard could hear someone ferreting around inside. He sat down and realized that it was in fact good to have a sit down. He looked around the garden at the Azaleas planted symmetrically all around it like a laager, but it was the view of the mountain peaks that he feasted his eyes on.

"You have a nice place here," he said as his eyes travelled down the valley, "a superb spot to build a house."

They talked about the environment for a few minutes until a stout woman appeared with a tea tray and some large slices of chocolate cake. Before long he was talking about his plans to go to England to study art.

"You're taking the sculpture with you?"

"Yes."

"On the plane?" He took the hand and weighed it in his two hands. "This weight, it will cost you a fortune."

Leonard hadn't thought about that, he had never travelled by air before.

"Look, I can stick another five hundred Rand on my offer, the Rand isn't going to get you very many British pounds. What do you say?"

Leonard sat wide-eyed, his heart beating fast, uncertainty written all over his face.

"Let's make it eleven thousand Rand," he heard the long-frowned man said.

The temptation was too much for him, and he caved in. "OK," he quaked.

When he left the house he had mixed emotions: elation at his ability to earn so much money at his age through his art work, the joy of being appreciated, but at the same time a sense of deep sadness that he was leaving a precious part of himself behind. As he stuck his hand in his pocket, and felt his camera, he consoled himself with the knowledge that he could still look at the photos he had taken of the hand and the painting of Lokkie before he left. He had also taken a photo of the rock-man, which had captured him all those hours until Lokkie came back, a kind of thank you, an acknowledgement for a favour done.

A stiff sea breeze sent a chill through him and he realized that the tide had turned; the breakers were swelling deep in the sea now leaving a large salt-scented beach covered with beautiful shells. Yes, he thought, and how the tide of his life had turned too, and that of his mother. He was barely six months in England after his European tour when the news came of his father's fatal heart attack and he had to go home. In the wink of an eye his father's life was spent, like a wave. Nothing left but the froth of his self-importance and striving for status. Suddenly he was free, and his mother too. She could come back to this lovely town, and he enrolled for a degree in Fine Arts at the University of Cape Town.

Leonard got up and shook the white sand off his pants. It was time to go home, his mother would have lunch ready. These end of term visits to her always seemed to pass too quickly and he still had his students' exam papers to mark when he got back to Cape Town. He thought of how fortunate he was to have got a post at the university as a junior lecturer soon after he had completed his degree. It enabled him, after a time, to set up his own small art gallery. His life was trotting along smoothly, pleasantly, no big highs or lows: friends, girl friend from time to time, art exhibitions, interesting things to do, all in all a good social life. Yes, life was good.

It was one of those days in the Cape when a white cloud rolling low over Table Mountain spread itself into the proverbial tablecloth. Leonard stood at the window looking at it, feeling that he could never tire of the sight. Reluctantly he turned away when his phone rang.

"Mr. Erasmus?" It was a cultured voice with a pleasant sound to it.

"Yes, speaking."

"My name is Ben Mynhard. I wonder if you could help me. I am looking for an artist by the name of Erasmus who sold a beautifully sculpted hand to my father around thirteen years ago. Might that by any chance be you?"

Leonard took the phone off the desk and sat down. A long forgotten feeling of loss surfaced in him and for a moment he thought that this could be an invitation for him to buy it back. Perhaps that pushy man had died and his son needed money.

"Yes, that's me."

"And there were two paintings as well, a landscape and a portrait. The portrait was named Lokkie."

Lokkie. The feeling of loss deepened as he thought of the photos – photos he seldom looked at: they were not the real things. He had wanted to keep that portrait. He wanted to remember her by it, the sweetness of their spontaneous, carefree lovemaking, and the first for her. For him it was a first that wasn't a schoolboy experimenting under peer pressure. Something so natural, beautiful and delicate, the likes of which he had not experienced since even with his sophisticated girl friends.

"Yes," he said, suddenly annoyed as the sense of longing contracted his heart, "What can I do for you?"

There was a moment of silence on the other end of the line, and when the voice came again it was clearly cautious.

"Mr. Erasmus, there's something I need to tell you, a promise I have made, but it's not something to talk about over the phone. Could we meet somewhere?"

The long lonely drive up to the Berg was a breathing space for Leonard. A space where he could at last let his feelings have their way. The last two weeks since he had met with Ben had been a time of tight control of thoughts and emotions. Once he had arranged time off from the university and Ben had made the arrangements with his father and Miriam for the meeting, he allowed his thoughts to wander. Chewing up mile after mile had the same effect on him as watching waves coming and going endlessly.

The first shock of hearing that he had a child had subsided. It had made way for something else, something that he could not put his finger on yet. Lokkie's child, a coloured child! The apartheid era might have disappeared into history, but in many people's minds, especially people like his father, it was as alive as if it had never died. Then another thought struck him: his mother, living out her peaceful life by the sea, serving her community with her grace and abilities, how would she feel about learning that she has a grand daughter, born from a Zulu girl? Instinctively he knew the answer to that: she would simply welcome her into her loving heart. That was how she was.

What about him, how did *he* feel about it, he asked himself? He had never considered himself a racist, and certainly when he made love to Lokkie it didn't even enter his mind. They were just two teenagers responding to what was natural to their bodies; not even thinking of consequences. But there were consequences, and the most tragic of all was that Lokkie, that delicate gentle girl, was murdered, murdered for the savings she had hoped would one day unite her with her child again. He wiped an obstinate tear from his cheek. A girl like that in a hell hole like Johannesburg!

The guilt wafted over him. Why didn't he go back to her after his father's death? Why didn't he at least go and see her? She must have been six, seven months pregnant by then! He clutched the steering wheel until his knuckles turned white. If he did, what would he have done? Married her? The lump in his throat refused to budge as mile after mile sped by, racing his thoughts. He opened the window as if they were clamouring to get out. Still they did not leave him.

He could not go on. He pulled up at the side of the road and switched the engine off. There it was in front of him: the wide sky spanning the immense space all around him. He put his arms on the steering wheel and buried his head in them. His body shook, and shook, and shook as raw sobs filled the landscape.

At last he lifted his head and looked at the trees swinging their arms gently to and fro like mothers rocking their hurt children.

"Lokkie", he said, "please forgive me, please, forgive me. I am so very sorry."

He heard the sound of a car in the distance and watched it in the rear view mirror getting bigger and bigger until it whizzed past him, then slowly getting smaller and smaller until it disappeared into the vastness of the country in front of him.

He realized that he must have been sitting there much longer than he thought, because the sun was hanging low in the sky. He started the car up and eased it onto the road.

His child, Miriam, what would she look like? Ben hadn't said, just that she was lovely, intelligent and a talented artist. What would he say to her when he met her? How would she feel about a father who had abandoned her mother, causing her to give her child away? Surely that must be what she was thinking. He wiped some moisture from his nose with the back of his hand, like he used to when he was a little boy. Amazing how life could be so smooth and comfortable one minute, he thought, and the next, just one 'phone call could change everything. The sun was setting, shooting pink rays through the clouds.

Leonard noticed that he was not far from Durban where he had planned to make a stopover. He wanted to be fresh and rested when he met Miriam, and he wanted first to go to the place where he had met Lokkie.

The next morning, after a substantial breakfast, he went out and bought a bunch of lilies. Their smell wafted around him as he was leaving the shop. He stopped suddenly, turned and went back to the counter.

"I want a big bunch of bright orange flowers," he said to the sales lady, "any kind, any mixture, just as long as they are orange."

Outside in the breeze the orange petals waved like winking arms, while the serene lilies stood firm against the moving air.

It was midday when he came to the place where the rock-man stood, unperturbed by human emotions, watching them play out their little dramas. He went down to the stream where Lokkie had led him when he asked for water, and put the flowers down on the grass. First he unwrapped the lilies, and one by one he floated them down the crystal clear stream. There were no thoughts in his mind; it was his *heart* honouring her, thanking her for the precious gift of a child.

When the last lily had floated away, he opened up the orange bunch. He felt they were a symbol of celebration, a celebration of Lokkie's short life. He arranged them in a vase he had bought in the florist and placed them on a little ledge protected from the wind on three sides. Stretched out on the grass he lingered a little longer watching their gaiety, then got up, brushed the dead grass off himself and walked back to where he had parked his car.

Through the little towns he drove to the other side of the mountain and after a bit of searching and a few wrong turns he found the house. As he got out of the car two dogs came out to greet him, a fat, plodding honey coloured one and a sprightly cinnamon coloured one, moving like a gazelle. He wondered whether the older one might be the puppy whose ears he had fondled all those years ago. The Azaleas, they were still there, now sturdy mature bushes touching each other with their leaves. The veranda was deserted.

Then he saw it: the hand! His hand! Welcoming him? His heart was thumping as he touched it, fingering the palm.

The French door onto the veranda opened and he looked up. She stepped out, Miriam, his child. He stood stunned, quite unable to believe his eyes. If it wasn't for the frizzy hair and the darker skin, it could have been his mother standing there. He remembered a photograph of her as a young girl, the spitting image of the girl standing in front of him. He was aware of her eyes scanning him. There was a confident penetrating look in them, which his mother's did not have. This girl was very much in charge of the situation. He felt as if she could see inside him, and that any pretence would be useless. There was nowhere for him to hide and he had a moment of intense panic that she might find him wanting. Then she smiled, and stepped forward pointing to the hand he realized he was still clutching, and said,

"Thank you for leaving your hand behind, it held mine when I felt lost and lonely."

For the first time he felt gratitude towards this Mr. Mynhard who pressurized him into selling it. He took both her hands in his and said:

"Now you have two hands to hold."

She said nothing but gave him a soft gentle smile, which was reminiscent of his mother's smile and the words just tumbled out:

"You look just like your grandmother."

"I have a grandmother?" There was excitement in her voice.

"Yes, a very beautiful grandmother. She will adore you." Her eyes lit up; two sparkling green pools.

Leonard had a sense that the whole house was listening, watching them out there on the veranda, so it was no surprise to him when the man who bought the hand came out, leaning heavily on his stick. He had aged, Leonard thought, but he looked less severe. He moved forward to shake hands with him as he had that first time they met, but the hand that took his then did not come up; it was hanging by his side, shaking in an effort to lift itself. He saw that it was lame and in a sudden flash of embarrassment let his drop as discretely as possible.

"You found the place easily?" the man enquired as he moved to sit down on the nearest chair, gesturing to a seat for Leonard.

"Fairly; not a great deal seems to have changed here, except everything has grown bigger," his hand took in the Azaleas with a wide circular sweep. He pointed to Honey. "Could this be the courageous pup that growled at me some fourteen years ago Mr. Mynhard?"

"The very same one, but fourteen years – unbelievable! It feels like yesterday. You must be tired? Thirsty? Lizzie will bring tea out soon. Do you need a wash?"

Leonard shook his head. "No thank you, I stopped off on the way, but a cup of tea will be most welcome."

"I believe you own a very successful art gallery?" Mr. Mynhard said.

"Yes, in Hanover Street, Sea Point."

"Ah, I know that area well – and you lecture at the university?"

"That's right. I was really lucky to have gotten a post there so soon after I graduated."

"Hmm. I don't think that sort of thing comes by luck – more a question of capability."

"Sometimes a combination of both," Leonard said, casting his eyes down, feeling slightly awkward. He saw the lame hand again. "I'm sorry about that," he said, pointing to it. "I did not realize…"

"Don't worry, in a few month's time it will be able to give you a proper handshake."

Leonard looked puzzled. "An injury? Did you have an accident?"

"No, it was a gradual deterioration, first of the legs, and then the hand, which one day just collapsed completely."

"Oh I *am* sorry! You say completely, yet – I see movement in it?"

"Ah, that is due to Miriam."

"Miriam?"

"Miriam has been doing some work with light on it and it is improving every day."

Leonard's jaw dropped. "Miriam is healing with light?"

He looked at her and saw a slight blush on her face; she seemed embarrassed by the focus on this aspect of herself.

"My God! Miriam, your grandmother has been doing healing work all her life and she often spoke of the light flowing through her, doing the work."

Miriam jumped up from her chair, her whole body vibrating with energy.

"My grandmother is a healer – with light?"

Leonard nodded. "Sure is."

She clapped her hands together like a little girl overjoyed by a longed for gift, and she reminded him of Lokkie and the children when he handed them the chocolate: hands clapped together twice before they opened it to receive the gift, a Zulu custom to signify gratitude. He swallowed at the thickness that had suddenly crept into his throat and hoped that the moisture in his eyes went unnoticed.

"Then she'll be able to tell me what... how – I mean, she'll be able to tell me all about it."

Leonard nodded again and Miriam made a little jig overwhelmed by her excitement. Cinnamon jumped up against her, barking. Honey struggled to her feet and knocked herself against Miriam's legs, not to be left out of the excitement, whatever it was about.

"Aunty Lizzie!"

She started for the house. Just then a coloured woman came out carrying a tea tray.

"Aunty Lizzie, my grandmother is a healer!"

Leonard watched the young woman as she put the tray carefully on the table before she took Miriam into her arms, and held her tight. So this was the woman Ben told him who brought Miriam up, the substitute for Lokkie. How very, very fortunate this child had been. He shuddered at the thought of how different it could have been – orphanage, or even if Lokkie had kept her, but he didn't want to entertain the guilty thoughts that surfaced. He looked at the sculpture that he had created, sitting unperturbed on the table, and the thought that he had when he carved it came into his mind: the hand of God. Was it the hand of God that preserved this beautiful gifted child? Perhaps even steered him to these mountains, and to Lokkie? A great calm came over him, and for a moment he was oblivious of his surroundings as in his mind's eye he reached out to the hand – like an act of surrender.

Mr. Mynhard's voice penetrated his musings. "We have a spare room ready for you if you'd like to stay over to-night?"

He shook his head, "Thank you, but I have made a booking at the nearby holiday resort. However I'd be grateful if I could come and see Miriam in the morning?"

Miriam was relieved when Mr. Bruno asked Aunty Lizzie to go into town that morning to do a few errands for him. He told Maria to tidy the house up early and then go to the laundry to see to the washing and to stay there until it was time to come and prepare lunch. She knew that he would disappear too. That's what she had always appreciated in Mr. Bruno: his respect for people's privacy. When Leonard's car drew up she saw him get into his buggy that could handle the rough terrain outside, and head in the direction of Filamon's vegetable patch.

She was surprised at how easy it was for her to be with this stranger who was her father. She showed him her artwork, introducing one piece at a time; carefully, like a cat exploring a new territory little by little. First she showed him the one where the sky and the mountain melted into each other. She watched him intently while he scrutinized it, watching that light around him that she saw

197

on first meeting him, growing brighter and bigger. Then she showed him the portrait of Ben with the frightened eyes. He didn't have to say anything, she could tell from the vibration of the light around him that he was excited.

"You certainly have talent!"

She slipped off her chair and disappeared into her bedroom, she came back a moment later carrying a framed picture which she put on the sideboard underneath the window where the light caught Lokkie's moist lips and lit up her eyes.

"So have you," she said.

She saw a shock wave going through him as if Lokkie's ghost had just appeared in the room. Sadness started to form around his mouth and he was silent. The room was silent. The moment was sacred. Then he pulled himself up straight.

"There *was* love, Miriam, those days we spent together were magical, beautiful. I did not know... we were so young, didn't think of consequences." He stopped abruptly, his eyes holding hers were pleading.

"If there was love, why didn't you go back to her?"

His breath was fast and shallow now. "I was on my way to England to study art, I told her so, she didn't seem to mind too much, she didn't think either that..."

"But you told her that you would remember her by that portrait, yet you sold it and it lay in a dusty outside room for over thirteen years."

He was near tears now and there was barely any light around him. "I didn't want to sell it, God knows I didn't, that and the hand, they were precious to me – but Mr. Mynhard offered me an enormous sum of money and I needed it for my study in England. I didn't know, I just didn't think..." His voice was cracking. "I sold my soul." He put his hand over his face turning away from her.

Miriam picked Lokkie's portrait up and took it back to her room, hanging it up carefully. She stood looking at it for a while thinking about what he had said. As she pondered, a wave of compassion washed over her, compassion for both her parents. *I am alive,* she thought, *they gave me life. Is that not precious?*

When she returned he had recovered himself.

"May I see more of your work?"

She thought of her eagle, but hesitated for a moment. Inside of her it was as if a coil was unravelling itself and she could feel the cells all over her body vibrating vigorously. When the sensation stopped, she went to her room and picked up the picture she had only shown to Ben.

There was her eagle, spreading its wings on the dining room table. She watched him, watched his eyes grow big and bright, as if a fire had been lit in them. A tiny twitch around his mouth seemed to shoot sparks with every movement.

"This one means a lot to you," his voice was soft, reverent.

"When I couldn't see the eagle in the sky, I looked at it here," she pointed to the picture. "It made me feel like I had wings and could fly away from anything that made me feel unhappy, even if it was only for a short while."

Spontaneously he took her in his arms and stroked her hair. She put hers around his neck and leaned her head on his chest.

"Will you let me take you to meet your grandmother?"

She let go of his neck suddenly and sprang back exuberantly.

"Of course, of course!"

In her excitement she knocked the eagle flying, floating to the floor, wings spread wide. As she stood looking down on it she had a sense of being carried on its wings, away, away to… somewhere deep, deepest within herself, and this time the coming of the voice felt as natural to her as her own breath:

This is home.

CPSIA information can be obtained
at www.ICGtesting.com
Printed in the USA
BVOW03s2052140417
481337BV00001B/24/P